"Carrie, are you sick?" The voice swam, rose higher, and dissolved in the roaring—a record running too fast. Pieces of glass. And out of the chaos then, all at once, a bit of land—a sunny, quiet rock—floated up, bobbed, and disappeared.

"Are you all right?"

"I'm okay. It was just a dizzy spell."

Lots of people had dizzy spells, she thought. People fainted. Once, in history class, Beth Cromwell had fallen right over, and afterward everybody said it was cramps. But this wasn't that, of course. This was something else. It scared her.

"An honest and gripping novel that lingers long in memory."

—ALA *Booklist,* starred review

THE LANGUAGE OF GOLDFISH

The Language of Goldfish

a novel by
ZIBBY ONEAL

I would like to give special thanks to Deborah Brodie for her help with this book. She has been both a fine editor and a good friend. **Z.O.**

Published by The Trumpet Club
666 Fifth Avenue, New York, New York 10103

Copyright © Zibby Oneal, 1980

ISBN 0-440-84784-2

This edition published by arrangement with Viking Penguin,
a division of Penguin Books USA Inc.
Set in Times Roman
Printed in the United States of America
February 1992

1 3 5 7 9 10 8 6 4 2
OPM

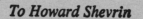
To Howard Shevrin

THE LANGUAGE OF GOLDFISH

◇ l ◇

Northpoint, Glenview, Golfside, Morton Grove. The train slowed smoothly, as if gliding on ribbon. A few people got off, a few got on, and cold air moved along the floor of the car.

Carrie sat looking at her reflection in the train's window and, beyond it, at the Morton Grove station. The station was contained within her reflected head like a thought.

Dead leaves were fluttering off the eaves troughs, blowing across the parking lot. Late October. Next month snow.

The train began to move again. The station slid backward and disappeared. Carrie bent forward and opened the book in her lap.

The paper smelled of school. The neat geometric figures lay solidly on the page. Permanent. Forever the square of the hypotenuse of a right-angle triangle would be equal to the sum of the square of the other two sides. Carrie liked that. She settled herself into the corner of the seat and began to study a new theorem.

By rights she should have been doing algebra. She was a

year ahead of herself, but the school was set up that way. If you were good at something, you could move ahead, and Carrie was good at math. She found it beautiful in its certainty. Unlike poetry, which bothered her, math was firm. Meanings didn't shift and change as they did in poetry, as they still sometimes did within her own head.

Carrie mouthed the theorem and closed her eyes, repeating again, memorizing.

The train moved and slowed and moved again. Each time it stopped, there was bustle in the aisle, momentary fresh air, and the sound of doors sliding shut. Carrie didn't look up until the conductor opened the door of the car and called, "Union Station next!" Then she pulled on her dark blue duffel coat and jammed the book into her book bag. She was first off when the train stopped.

Steam hissed from under the cars, stale smelling, and clouded the cold air above the platform. For a moment Carrie stopped and watched the steam rise and umbrella over her; then she hitched the book bag more firmly onto her shoulder and started up the ramp. Under the vast glass and marble arch of the station she turned left and headed toward the cab stand. "One eighty North Michigan," she said. And then, "Please!"

The cabdriver turned to look at her and pushed down the handle of his meter. "Right."

The buildings on either side formed a canyon through which the taxi moved. They crossed Canal Street, heading north. Carrie put a stick of gum into her mouth and chewed. Like a normal teenager, she thought. Almost normal. Going where? To the dentist was probably what the cabdriver thought.

The elevator at 180 North Michigan scared Carrie every time. It shivered as it rose, threatening to shake itself apart, she thought, leaving her to make a slow fall down the shaft. She always imagined the fall as a leisurely descent past elevator cables and the closed doors of other floors—a dream fall. And, as in a dream, she could never catch hold of anything to stop herself.

She stood in the lobby, pressed the "Up" button, and waited for the elevator to tremble its way down to her. The lobby was deserted. During the first weeks she'd come to see Dr. Ross, Carrie had dreaded arriving and leaving—the time spent in the lobby and in the elevator—for fear she would meet someone she knew. The Institute was on the twenty-third floor—the whole twenty-third floor—so that anyone in the elevator who saw her press that button would know where she was going and that she had been unwell.

"Unwell" was her mother's term. "Your illness" was another. Like so many of her mother's terms for things, these prettied the truth. They made it something her mother could handle. People in Northpoint did not have crazy children.

The elevator doors slid apart. Carrie stepped in, pressed "23," and tried not to notice the shivering. Instead she concentrated on what she would talk about with Dr. Ross. She imagined the familiar water stain on the ceiling in his office, which had, from the first, reminded her of a rabbit,

and she began to assemble a first sentence.

◦2◦

In the beginning, in the hospital, it had been harder to talk. Partly, Carrie had not known what to say. Partly, she had not wanted to say it. She had wanted to let her head float. But Dr. Ross would not permit it. He pulled her back, reeled her in with questions. "Tell me when you think it started."

"How do I know when it started?" Carrie remembered saying irritably. It wasn't as if on some particular morning she'd suddenly felt different. Things didn't happen that way. They changed slowly. You went along more or less the same until one day you knew something was terribly wrong. And then you realized it had been that way for a very long time.

"There was a morning in September. I was lying in bed listening to Sophie get breakfast. Sophie's our maid. I always hear her starting breakfast in the morning just before my alarm goes off.

"It was a Tuesday. I remember because I was thinking there were still four more days of Sylvester that week. Sylvester Country Day School. That's where all the rich kids in Northpoint go."

In the bathroom the shower had been running, Carrie remembered. Moira washing her hair. Carrie and Moira

6

shared a bathroom between them—literally between—
Moira's room was on one side, Carrie's on the other. Carrie
reached over and pushed in the alarm. There was no point
getting up until Moira had finished. Her hair took a long
time.

Carrie lay on her back and hated her wallpaper. She
imagined staring it off the wall—the silly pink bouquets
curling up, shriveling, dropping off like leaves—so that
when Sophie came up to vacuum, the carpet would be lit-
tered with withered bouquets. "After all, it's autumn, Sophie." Carrie smiled. But of course it would be no joke.
Mrs. Gooch, the decorator, and Carrie's mother had spent
hours choosing that particular paper.

"You'd better get up. It's past seven-thirty." Moira
stood in the doorway, turbaned in one towel, wrapped in
another. "What are you going to wear?"

Carrie shrugged.

"Well, can I borrow your green shetland?"

"Sure," Carrie said. "I don't care. Just don't stretch it."

"What?"

"I mean with your enormous chest."

"Don't be gross," Moira said, then came into the room
and began rummaging in Carrie's closet.

"It's on the chair, under my books."

"You really don't care what happens to your clothes, do
you?" said Moira.

"Not really." Carrie rolled over, sat up, and put her feet
on the floor. She sat looking out the window, scratching.
Across the street the windows in Mrs. Padmore's house

7

caught fire with early sunlight. Mrs. Padmore was dead. Her maid had told Carrie that, on the day Mrs. Padmore died, she'd actually seen her soul disappear, had seen it fly straight out the attic window. "Ridiculous," Carrie's mother said. "That's maid talk." Probably. But if it *had* happened, Carrie thought, she'd have given anything to see it.

"Do you suppose Mrs. Padmore's soul really flew, Moira?"

"Of course not. Hurry up," her sister said.

"You used to think so."

"That was five *years* ago. I was ten."

"I still think so."

"Fine. Listen, it's almost twenty of."

Carrie pulled open a bureau drawer and took out underwear. "Do you ever think about the goldfish, Moira?"

"Carrie, for God's sake!"

"Well, do you?"

"No. What's to think about? Look, do you want to miss the whole first hour?"

"But remember how we used to whistle to them?"

"Carrie, quit it, will you?"

Then Moira turned on her hair dryer, and its noise drowned out any further conversation. Carrie began dressing.

It was silly to have brought up the goldfish. Moira was impatient in the morning. If Carrie wanted to talk about things they'd done years ago together, the time to do it was at night. When Moira was half asleep, she'd talk about any-

8

thing, but on school mornings she was uptight. Moira hated being late, hated breaking any rule. She always had.

Carrie pulled a sweater over her head and found her kilt hanging on the closet doorknob. She stood at the bathroom mirror, running a comb through her no-color hair. After today there were only three more days until the weekend. Only—how many more weeks till summer? She thought about the bright, hot corridors at Sylvester where in less than an hour she would be elbowing her way to English class. She thought of the other kids, and her stomach began to ache a little. Her stomach often ached a little lately.

Moira had gone downstairs. Carrie put the comb away, gathered her books, and followed.

Their mother was already at the breakfast table. Duncan was stirring his cereal around and around absentmindedly, concentrating on his list of fifth-grade spelling words. Moira glanced up quickly as Carrie walked in. Their mother seemed to have paused in mid-sentence, dangling a saccharine tablet above her coffee. Carrie slid into her chair. They'd been talking about her.

"Carrie, we've got to do something about your hair," her mother said. "It needs a shaping."

Carrie nodded, reached for the sugar and sprinkled some on her cornflakes.

"What do you think, Moira? About an inch shorter, too?" Her mother was studying her through slitted eyes, appraising, and Carrie bent to eat.

"I'll see about getting an appointment for Saturday."

"Saturday morning I go to Mrs. Ramsay's."

"Oh, right. Well, Saturday afternoon then."

"We might go to the Art Institute Saturday afternoon if Mrs. Ramsay can find a sitter."

Her mother sighed and lowered the saccharine into her coffee. Carrie spooned up cornflakes, hoping something would divert her mother's attention. She imagined it like a laser beam, riveting first one of them and then another with concern. Carrie didn't care about her hair. She cared about her Saturday morning drawing lesson.

Mrs. Ramsay taught art at Sylvester. Saturdays she gave Carrie a private lesson because, as she said, Carrie had talent. Carrie hadn't thought her parents would agree to let her drop the Saturday morning tennis clinic at the club for drawing lessons, but, surprisingly, they had. She loved the lessons—they were the best part of the week.

"Carrie, hurry up and finish." Moira was craning out of her chair to see the kitchen clock.

"I'll try for a Friday appointment," their mother said, "but if I can't get one, you'll just have to skip your lesson this week."

"I can't do that. Mrs. Ramsay's expecting me."

"You can call her."

"No." Carrie felt the knot in her stomach tighten.

Her mother leaned back against the polished wood of her chair, straightened her place mat with her fingertips. "Don't make a fuss, Carrie."

"I can't miss my lesson. Drawing is very important to me."

"Well, I'm not asking you to give up drawing. Just one lesson, for Heaven's sake."

"I can't." Carrie stood up and started toward the door.

Her mother looked abstracted, as if she hadn't heard. Instead, she reached for the stack of mail beside her plate, riffled through it, and pulled out a check paper-clipped to an envelope. "Before I forget, the announcement about the junior dances came from school. I've written a check you can take to the secretary."

Carrie looked at her mother incredulously. "But we talked about that! I told you I didn't want to go to those dances."

"Moira and I've discussed it. All the eighth graders go. We think you'll like them once you get started."

Carrie turned to look at Moira. "Moira agrees with you?"

"She loved the dances."

"I'm not Moira."

Her mother handed her the check. "I'm afraid Daddy and I are going to insist. It's time you began doing these things, Carrie."

"And," Carrie had said in the hospital, looking away from Dr. Ross, "that's the first time it happened."

It was curiously hard to explain what had happened. In a way, it didn't seem like much of anything. A dizzy spell. But at the same time Carrie had known from the beginning, without really knowing, that it was something worse than being dizzy.

"It seemed as though things suddenly slipped sideways," she said. "Inside my head colors—queer colored shapes—began to tumble around like the colored glass in a kaleidoscope. There was a kind of roaring noise. My head began to float. I thought I was sick. I thought I was going to faint.

"I held onto the doorframe and shut my eyes. Behind my eyes I saw the colors all beautiful and tumbling. And then it was over and Moira was telling me to hurry up."

◦ 3 ◦

There had been so many appointments now. Carrie shifted her book bag on her shoulder and watched the lighted numbers blink one after another as the elevator rose.

She remembered the leaves in the street that morning, elm mostly, some maple. She'd scuffed in them, sending them fluttering ahead. "Moira," she'd said, "how come you agreed with Mother?"

"Because she's right, Carrie. You really *should* go to the dances."

Carrie watched the leaves flutter up, flutter down. "But isn't it my business?"

Moira didn't answer.

"Isn't it, Moira?" Carrie turned to look at her sister. Moira's face was turning pink in the chilly air. A strand of blond hair had come loose from behind her ear and blew

12

against her cheek. Carrie reached out and touched her shoulder. "Moira?"

"Carrie, quit it, will you?" Moira shrugged her hand off irritably. Carrie looked down at her mittens.

"You can't go on being a little kid forever," Moira said flatly, and she began to walk faster. Carrie nodded, watching the leaves on the sidewalk flutter and tumble like colored glass in a kaleidoscope. She began feeling dizzy again.

"I don't think I can go to school today," she said suddenly. "I think I'm sick."

Moira looked at her, exasperated. "You were all right before."

"I got dizzy after breakfast. It must be flu."

Moira stood, torn between concern and impatience. "You'd better go home then. I'll get your assignments." And she started to run.

Carrie watched until Moira, flapping legs and scarf and book bag, had disappeared around the corner, and then she turned toward home. Sophie was in the kitchen cleaning up after breakfast. "I'm getting sick," Carrie told her. "I'm staying home."

Sophie settled a plate in the dishwasher and surveyed her. "You don't look so good. Better go lie down."

Carrie nodded. She climbed the stairs, undressed, and crawled into her unmade bed. She pulled the blanket up to her chin and felt with her feet for a cool, smooth place in the sheets. Then she waited for more symptoms of flu.

First hour would have begun. English. Carrie could imagine it. She sat behind Katherine Fowles in English, in front of Laura Mott. Across the aisle was Jerome Taylor, who had acne.

Katherine was fat—terribly, grossly fat. Laura was beautiful. Sometimes Carrie thought Mrs. Gordon had put all the losers together in one section—Jerome and Katherine and herself—but then there was Laura, which ruined the theory.

Carrie pictured Katherine's fat back in front of her and Laura shoving a folded note into her hand to pass across the aisle to Beth Marshall. She was glad not to be there.

She flopped over. School in Chicago had been different. But that was elementary school and I was little, Carrie thought, and lots of things were different.

They'd lived in Hyde Park, close to the hospital where her father was a resident. Duncan had been a baby then. Carrie and Moira had learned to roller-skate on the sidewalk outside the emergency room, had jumped rope, had drawn hopscotch boards there with colored chalk. Sidewalks were the first thing she missed when they moved to Northpoint.

"There'll be grass," her mother had said. Carrie could remember the eager expression on her face. "And we'll live in a house instead of an apartment, and Daddy will have his own office." All of this turned out to be true. But Carrie had missed Hyde Park so much that for weeks her stomach ached.

Northpoint was all strangeness. The new house echoed with the voices of painters. For the first time in their lives she and Moira slept in separate rooms. During the day they wandered in the house or in the yard with only each other

14

for company. It was that summer they invented the goldfish language.

Carrie heard the roar of the dishwasher and then Sophie coming slowly upstairs on her bad leg. Sophie was fat. She had varicose veins, which hurt her more some days than others. She looked in at Carrie's door. "Feeling better?"

Carrie nodded. She was thinking of the fish pond at the bottom of the garden.

They'd found it the first day, murky green, surrounded by junipers. In the center of the pond someone had built an island of rocks, too far from the edge for them to reach. The rocks were moss covered. Slimy green algae clung to them just under the water's surface. Moira had leaned out as far as she dared, trying to touch the island with the handle of a broom, but it wasn't possible. "It's too far," she said.

She and Carrie flopped down on their stomachs and looked at the island and the dim green water. A leaf was spinning on the surface. "If we were really tiny," Carrie had said, "we could use that leaf for a boat. We could paddle it out to the island."

"Like Thumbelina," said Moira.

"We could live there," said Carrie.

And then all at once in the dim water they had seen a flash of brightness. "Fish!" They watched and counted half a dozen.

Moira went to get soda crackers. She and Carrie crumbled them on the surface of the pond. Then Moira did a funny thing. Leaning far out over the pond, gripping the side, she began to whistle softly. "You'll fall in," Carrie said, then stopped, for slowly, one by one, the goldfish had begun to rise through the scummy water. Carrie held her breath. They were enormous. Their tails rippled like silk, and their mouths opened and closed, snapping crumbs. "See? Magic," Moira said. "They heard me calling them."

Every day that first hot summer they went to the pond with crackers for the fish. They watched the crumbs float on the surface. They lay flat and whistled and watched the fish rise in response to their call.

"If we wanted, the goldfish could carry us out to the island on their backs," Moira said. "If we asked them, I mean."

"Why don't we?" Carrie whispered, only half in doubt.

"I just made that up, Carrie. It wouldn't really happen."

"They come when we call them."

"That's different."

Carried looked at the orange-gold backs of the darting fish. "If we lived on the island, we'd never have to move," she said. "We could just live there forever. Things would always stay the same."

"What would we eat?" Moira had answered. "Algae?"

Carrie pressed her cheek into the pillow and stared at the wall. When school started things had begun to change even faster. Moira started walking home from school every day with new friends and Carrie tagged along, listening to them talk but not always understanding what they said. She looked over the other kids in her class. They all seemed the same to her. More and more she thought about her old

16

neighborhood, and about her friend Tanya Abraham, who could spit through the gap in her front teeth.

Remembering all that made Carrie sad. She closed her eyes and thought about the fish, and after a while she fell asleep.

When she woke it was late afternoon. In the next room Moira's stereo was playing softly. From down the hall came the irregular thump of Duncan's weights. Carrie felt fine. The morning seemed far away and unreal. When her father said at dinner that her long sleep must have cured her, she thought that probably it was just that simple and that he was right.

◊ **4** ◊

It didn't happen again for quite a while. September passed. The weather turned colder, and the days were full of small busy things. Carrie forgot.

She went back to school the next day with a written excuse signed by her father. She had to take it to Mr. Adderley's office before first hour began, and consequently she was late for class.

She slid into her seat behind Katherine Fowles and glanced up at the board. Mrs. Gordon was talking to a student. Carrie stowed her math and ancient-history books under her seat and got out her English notebook. Katherine turned around. "You missed a quiz yesterday," she said.

"I was sick."

"What did you have? A cold or what?"

"Flu, I guess."

"You got over it fast."

Carrie looked at Katherine, loathing her pale, fat face. Katherine's eyes were like raisins wedged into bread dough. "Wonder drugs," Carrie said.

"I never heard of anyone getting over the flu that fast."

"Well, now you have."

"I bet you weren't even sick."

"You want to mind your own business, Katherine?" Carrie opened the notebook and took a ballpoint out of her bag.

"Well, excuse *me!*" Katherine said. "Aren't *we* sensitive!"

Carrie ignored her. Fat lump. She looked around the classroom, watched a note travel down the row next to her, and saw Martha Grant lean out to take it. Martha was another of the beautiful ones. She turned around and smiled at someone in the back of the room, reminding Carrie of a girl in a Florida grapefruit commercial. They all reminded her of somebody like that, except, of course, for a few people like Katherine.

Mrs. Gordon was at her desk. She leafed through her text and said, "Page 184, 'The Eve of St Agnes.' " Around the room books cracked. "John Keats was a very great English poet," said Mrs. Gordon. Carrie flipped to page 184. Mrs. Gordon began to read:

18

"St Agnes' Eve—Ah, bitter chill it was!
The owl, for all his feathers, was a-cold;
The hare limped trembling through the frozen grass, . . ."

Carrie looked out the window. She followed the course of a falling leaf until it had spun past the sill and disappeared. She wondered how she might draw that slow descent, all the spin and flutter. Mrs. Ramsay had shown her a print once in which some painter—Balla?—had tried to paint his impression of the movements a dog made walking. To Carrie, it hadn't looked like a dog walking.

Mrs. Gordon kept on. Carrie had read the poem the night before. She'd liked the colors in it, especially the lines describing how the colors of the stained glass fell on the girl's bed.

Mrs. Gordon read:

"They told her how, upon St Agnes' Eve,
Young virgins might have visions of delight,
And soft adorings from their loves receive . . ."

Someone snorted quietly behind Carrie, and then Katherine Fowles, of all people, began to giggle. Mrs. Gordon put the book down and stared. "Perhaps you'd like to explain to the class what you find so amusing, Katherine."

Katherine ducked her head. The room was silent. Carrie could see her blushing. Even the back of her neck was flushed. The fat, loathsome thing. It was the word "virgin," of course, and the "soft adorings from their loves." Carrie looked down at her book, ruffled the pages. She felt vaguely embarrassed, as she had in elementary school when some child accidentally wet his pants. And she felt something else, too. The words made her uncomfortable in a way she couldn't identify.

"I don't know why I laughed," Katherine said miserably. She mumbled it into her book.

"Well, I don't believe Keats intended any jokes in this poem. Arthur Stillwell, can you explain the poem thus far to those who think it's humorous?"

Carrie shifted in her seat. What did Katherine know about soft adorings? Did she think about things like that? Carrie looked back at the window, trying to remember the motion the leaf had made, because she felt uneasy and strange. She wished Mrs. Gordon would go on to another poem.

At lunch they teased Katherine. Melissa Post, who sat each day at the table with the popular girls, leaned back in her chair and called to Katherine, "Who did you have in mind this morning? Jim Clark?" It was a joke, but of course Katherine didn't understand.

She began to get red. "Somebody," she said. "Nobody's business."

"Somebody we don't know about? Some big romance?"

"That's for me to know and you to find out."

Why doesn't she just keep quiet? Carrie thought. If you keep quiet they leave you alone.

"Is he going to be at the dances, Katherine?" Melissa rocked back in her chair and grinned at her friends.

"Maybe yes. Maybe no."

20

Dumb Katherine. Her upper lip had begun to perspire.

"Come on and tell us," Melissa insisted.

"Wait and see." Katherine smiled but it didn't work well.

"Why don't you shut up?" Carrie said quietly, under her breath. But Katherine heard. She leaned forward across the table and stared at Carrie. "You take that back," she said softly. "Who do you think you are, anyway, telling me to shut up?"

Carrie shook her head. "I didn't mean it the way it sounded." But Katherine was too angry to pay attention. She leaned forward until her damp white face almost touched Carrie's.

"You creep," she whispered fiercely. "If you weren't Moira Stokes's sister you wouldn't be anything at all."

Carrie stood up. She wanted to get out of the lunchroom.

In the outer hall she stood a minute, catching her breath, and then she went out and stood on the fire escape. The cool air felt good. Technically, the fire escape was off limits, but she didn't care at that moment. She took a deep breath and shook herself. She guessed she didn't mind too much what Katherine had said. It was true in a way, at least as far as the kids at Sylvester were concerned. She sat down on the metal steps and hugged her knees.

One fall she and Tanya had bought a bag of marbles from Marvin Byrd, not because they knew how to play but because the colored glass was beautiful. They'd spread them out on the windowsill in Tanya's room, and the sunlight shining through the glass had made colored splotches on the rug. Carrie sat, remembering, hugging her knees, and then suddenly knew why she'd remembered just then. It was because of the lines about the colors of stained glass in "The Eve of St Agnes."

She stood up and kicked an acorn off the fire escape. She didn't want it to be because of that. She hated that poem now. She hated Katherine for giggling. She hated the queer feeling the poem gave her. She didn't want her thoughts about Tanya mixed up with any of that.

◊ 5 ◊

On Saturday morning Carrie walked the ten blocks to Mrs. Ramsay's with two inches less hair. The fuss had been for nothing. Somebody named Genevieve in a pink silky smock had cut it Friday afternoon.

It was a perfect October morning. The elms had begun to look bare, but the maples were still turning. Here and there people were loading station wagons to drive into Evanston for the Northwestern game. Carrie's parents were doing that. She'd left her father in the kitchen mixing whiskey sours to take along, squeezing lemons, littering the sink, and making Sophie cross.

At the corner by the Standard station, she turned left toward Mrs. Ramsay's. The street was scattered with wind-fall apples, and Carrie sent one skittering ahead along the blacktop. It had a lovely cidery smell.

She walked slowly, wanting every part of the morning to last as long as possible. She loved Saturdays. They made up for the rest of the week.

Mrs. Ramsay's house was small and close to the Village. The yards around the houses on her block were not so big as on Carrie's street or so well cared for, but there was something gay and friendly about them and about the houses themselves. Carrie felt at home here.

Noah Ramsay opened the door. His mouth was smeared with jam. "My dad's gone to Cleveland," he said matter-of-factly. Behind him Saskia, his twin, stood holding a huge, still-wet finger painting, rattling it to attract Carrie's attention.

"It's of all the leaves in our yard," she said, "and our dog before he died. I'm hanging it on the fridge."

"If that's Carrie, let her in," Mrs. Ramsay called.

The twins stood back and held the door open. Carrie stepped around the paint jars and into the living room. It was bright with sunlight.

"Sit down, Carrie. I'll be right there. I'm making tea," Mrs. Ramsay called above the roar of the washing machine.

Carrie looked around her. She loved the room—the sun streaming through the windows onto the faded slipcovers, the rug worn and strewn with the children's toys. She felt utterly comfortable.

Mrs. Ramsay came out of the kitchen, drying her hands on the back of her blue jeans. "It'll be ready in a second," she said. "But listen, Carrie. I have a terrific idea for you. I got a notice at school about a competition I think you should enter."

She perched on the arm of the sofa and looked up at Carrie. Her eyes were the color of fog. Tiny wrinkles fanned out at their edges, but they were like squint wrinkles or laugh wrinkles, not wrinkles that had to do with age.

"It's open to all junior-high art students," Mrs. Ramsay was saying. "What do you think? Do you have enough for a portfolio?"

"I don't know," Carrie said. "Not enough that are good maybe."

"Well, the thing to do is to bring all your drawings next time and we can decide. Actually, you'd have time to do some new ones if you worked hard." Then she grinned. "Will you look at this house? They called and offered me the *Good Housekeeping* award, but I turned it down. I don't want to make all the Northpoint ladies jealous."

Carrie laughed.

"What award?" said Noah. "Tell me."

Mrs. Ramsay stood up. She shoved a straggle of hair behind her ear. "I'm teasing. Now you two run along so Carrie and I can work."

They went into the dining room, and Carrie spread out her sketchbook on the table while Mrs. Ramsay got the teapot. "So what about the competition?" Mrs. Ramsay said. "I have to file for you."

Carrie drew a circle with her finger on the table. "I guess it'd be okay," she said. "I might as well enter if I can get the drawings together."

"Good. That's what I think." Mrs. Ramsay handed her a cup of tea. "So let's see what you've done."

Carrie opened her sketchbook. Mrs. Ramsay looked at the first new drawing, squinted, rubbed at a charcoal line with her thumb. "You've got something wrong with the perspective here."

"That's the way it looked to me."

"Well, okay then, if that's how you see it. Your way of looking is as good as mine."

"No, it's not."

"Honey, I've told you a hundred times, that's what art is all about. You don't want to see the way anyone else sees. You want to use your own eyes."

"Why don't you say that in class? At school?"

"Ah—school." Mrs. Ramsay frowned. "It would be pointless. Those kids—most of them—don't even know they've *got* eyes. If I told them to use their own eyes to see—really see—they wouldn't know what I meant."

"So I'm going to leave this the way it is," Carrie said.

Mrs. Ramsay chuckled. "You do that."

Saturday mornings seemed both to last forever and to be over in an instant. Sometimes Mrs. Ramsay made suggestions, sometimes she didn't. Often the two of them sat for an hour or longer working without speaking. Sunlight would move across the table, touching first the edges of the drawing paper, melting slowly across it, running down onto the floor before the kitchen door. It was the only way Carrie was aware that time passed.

But today Mrs. Ramsay talked more. She seemed edgy.

Finally she put down her charcoal pencil and said, "No use. I can't do a thing. We've got to stop earlier than usual, I'm sorry to say. I've got something to do." Then she looked at Carrie. "I didn't call about going to the Art Institute. I can't today. I thought you'd know if I didn't call."

"I sort of thought that. It's okay."

Carrie *had* thought that. It hadn't been firm. She hadn't really expected they'd go when Mrs. Ramsay didn't call. All the same, she was disappointed.

Walking home, she tried not to feel cross with Mrs. Ramsay. People got busy. There were other days to go. It was as her mother said, Mrs. Ramsay was doing her a favor. She was a teacher, not a friend. Except that she *was* a friend, Carrie thought in confusion. She was Carrie's best friend now. Carrie had had only one other best friend—Tanya Abraham—and that was a long time ago in Hyde Park.

Carrie crossed at the corner by the Standard station. The whole afternoon lay ahead, and she was free to do anything.

She could go through her drawings—that was one thing. She could go through the old ones or start something new— the leaf spinning past the window in English class, for instance. Not the leaf but the movement itself. Leave out the leaf altogether and draw the movement. She imagined circles within circles gradually growing larger. It appealed to her to leave out the body of the leaf—all the confusion of its physical appearance—and draw only the geometry of its fall. She began to hurry.

"Moira!" she yelled, slamming the back door. "Guess what?"

Sophie was sitting at the kitchen table resting her leg. "Moira's got a boy over," she said.

"Who do you mean?" Carrie stopped short with all her news about the competition and the new drawing still in her throat.

"I wouldn't know. Some boy is all I saw."

Carrie dropped her sketchbook on the table and listened. She could hear their voices coming from the library. Moira had never had a boy over before. It made the house seem strange.

"Do you want a sandwich?" Sophie asked. "The others had their lunch."

Carrie took the sandwich outside. She wandered down to the bottom of the garden, away from the house. There were leaves floating on the surface of the pond. Carrie lay down and watched them move lazily toward the little island, propelled by an air current she couldn't even feel.

The fish were gone. They lived all winter in a tank in the cellar. She had helped her father sieve them out in September. Still, out of habit, she leaned over and whistled quietly, ruffling the water with the old goldfish language. Then she blew harder, sent a leaf spinning wildly. Halfway across, it caught water and sank.

If you watch very closely, you can see that nothing holds still, Carrie thought. Not leaves or water or even people. Duncan needed new pants again. Sophie, on her birthday, would be half a century old. And Moira was drifting away someplace, spinning away like a bright yellow leaf.

Carrie stared at the reflection of her face on the water.

She wanted it to hold still, stay that way. But even while she watched, the water rippled and her reflection broke apart and joggled in disconnected fragments on the surface.

◦ 6 ◦

Three days a week, after school, Carrie played field hockey. Miss Barnes had moved her from right back to center in September because she was fast, but also, Carrie suspected, because she never missed a practice. She was almost the only one who never missed. The other girls got excuses from the nurse as often as they could. If the nurse kept track, Carrie thought, she'd realize some of them were getting excuses two or three times a month.

In early November it was nearly twilight when practice ended. And it was cold. Carrie's fingers felt permanently stiffened around her hockey stick by five o'clock. She started across the field toward the school behind a group of other players. "Take showers and warm up before you go home," Miss Barnes shouted after them, just as she had advised showers to cool off in September.

The locker room was thick with steam before Carrie had her shin pads off. There were four showers, all in use. Carrie waited. She didn't mind waiting. In fact, she purposely took her time. Dressing and undressing for gym made her uncomfortable. Girls pretended not to look at one another, but she knew they did. They compared. Besides, if she didn't hurry she could go by her father's office at just about the time he was leaving and ride home with him.

"Are you next for the shower, Carrie?"

"Go ahead."

Melissa Post and Jane Stevens were shouting at each other between shower stalls. Carrie stuffed her shin pads into her locker. Susan Rogers came out of the shower wrapped in a towel. "Carrie, did you understand what Mr. Crawford was talking about today?" she asked.

Of course she had. It was math. "You mean the new part he did on the board?"

"Yes. I don't get it."

"Do you want me to show you?"

"If you wouldn't mind. Do you have time?"

Carrie spread out her math book on a bench. "It isn't very hard. Look."

Susan frowned. She followed Carrie's explanation, moving her lips. "You see?" said Carrie.

"I don't see why you moved the X."

"To balance the equation. Watch."

They went through it again, the whole problem. Susan nodded. "I still don't get it," she said. "Maybe I can just skip over that part."

"Not if you want to understand what's going on the rest of the year."

Susan looked up. "It's easy for you, isn't it?"

"Pretty much."

"Boy, I wish it was for me! If my math grade goes down any further, my father'll probably send me to boarding school or something."

"No, he won't." Carrie smiled.

She had seen Susan's father at Lower School Music Night, had watched his face while Susan played a flute solo. She remembered because she wondered how you'd draw that expression, all lighted up from someplace behind his eyes. Susan had played really badly. The expression did not have to do with the music. He loved her, that was all.

"If *he* doesn't, my mother'll probably make him. She'd love to get me in boarding school."

"Why don't you ask Mr. Crawford tomorrow? He can explain it better than I can."

"Yeah, well, I suppose I could do that," Susan said vaguely. She got up and began taking clothes out of her locker.

The room was slowly emptying. There was a free shower, and Carrie started toward it, then changed her mind, realizing it had gotten late and she'd miss her father if she didn't hurry.

The cold air felt wonderful after the steam in the locker room. Carrie breathed deeply just for the pleasure of it and headed down Hartman toward her father's office. The air was blue. The streetlights along Hartman came on suddenly, all at once, as if somewhere in a remote building a man in overalls glanced at the sky, decided it was dark enough, and flipped a switch.

The balls of light seemed to tug at the lampposts like

balloons trying to escape into air. Carrie looked at them and imagined a drawing. She saw drawings every place now. Since she had begun trying to draw the circling fall of the elm leaf, the idea of making patterns in which the real object disappeared obsessed her. She no longer drew the thing itself. She had half a dozen new drawings to enter in the competition in which patterns of motion had replaced the body of the object entirely.

Just ahead was the Northpoint Clinic. Carrie walked more quickly. She went through the front door and up the stairs to the second floor. Miss Phelps was straightening magazines in the waiting room when Carrie came in.

Her father was already in his coat.

"I almost missed you," Carrie said.

Her father smiled. "But you didn't." Then he offered Miss Phelps a ride.

Carrie felt unreasonably disappointed. She had nothing against Miss Phelps really. She was all right in a fussy, nervous sort of way. It was just that Carrie liked riding home alone with her father.

They dropped Miss Phelps at her corner and turned back the other way toward home. Carrie moved over and put her books on the seat. "The reason I was late," she said, "is that I had to show Susan Rogers how to do the math assignment. She's terrible at math."

Carrie's father chuckled gently. "I'll bet she is."

"She can't figure out a thing. Even after I explained it twice, she didn't understand."

"Well, she's a pretty little girl. She'll never have to understand. Nobody'll ever care whether she can add two and two.''

"Yeah." Carrie looked out the window for a moment at the lighted houses along Goodman. Then she said, "Did I tell you Mrs. Ramsay wants me to enter a drawing competition? I'm the only person in any of her art classes she's going to enter.''

"Well, that's fine, isn't it?"

"I probably won't win. I probably won't even get honorable mention, but I think it's good experience.''

"Sure it is.''

"I've been working on some new drawings. I guess you'd call them abstract—I don't know. I had an idea about drawing just movement, leaving out the other details. I could show you better than I can explain.''

"I'd like to see them sometime.''

"We could look at them before dinner.''

They were almost home. Her father turned into their street. He stopped in the driveway beside the back door. "Want to get out before I pull into the garage?''

Carrie got out and went into the house. She carried her books upstairs to her room. Duncan's television cast a bluish light into the hall. Moira was talking on the phone. Carrie took her new sketches from the closet and spread them on her desk. Of the six, there were three she liked best: the leaf done two different ways, and one of the surface of the pond breaking into ripples.

They were good. Carrie was as certain of that as she was

when she'd solved an equation. In a way, doing the drawings had been like solving an equation, neat and certain and clean.

She carried the drawings downstairs carefully, using both hands, as if they were breakable. Her parents were in the library having a drink. Her mother looked soft and pretty in the lamplight in a pale yellow cashmere sweater. "I brought the drawings down," Carrie said.

"Which drawings, dear?"

"I was telling Daddy about them. They're to enter in a competition."

"Spread them out here under the light." Her father shoved a stack of papers to one side of the desk. Carrie laid the drawings side by side on the mahogany surface. They looked beautiful.

"Well," her father said, "I see what you mean by abstract."

Her mother stood up and leaned over the desk. "But, Carrie, what are they pictures *of*?" she said.

"That one's a leaf I saw floating down past a window at school. It was spinning. I've tried to show that, you see? Just the movement?"

"Are they *all* leaves?"

"No. That one's the pond. When the surface breaks?"

Carrie's father nodded. Her mother was still bending over the pictures, frowning. She looked, Carrie thought, the way Susan had, trying to understand the equation. "You know," her mother said, "I have trouble understanding art.

Remember the winter Georgina got someone to lecture to a group of us at the Art Institute? I never could see what I was supposed to."

"It's just the movement—" Carrie began. Then she stopped.

"They're very interesting," her father said.

"I thought you might like to see them. They're no big deal. Just an idea I had." Suddenly she felt clumsy, as if her body had grown huge and ungainly. She leaned over the desk and gathered the pictures together awkwardly with fingers that had become thick stubs. "Anyway," she said, "I'll see you at dinner."

She looked back into the library on her way upstairs. Her father was making himself another drink. Her mother had begun again on her needlepoint, and they were already talking about something else.

◦ 7 ◦

Carrie woke with something nagging her. She lay still, turned her face into the pillow, and tried to think what it was that was on her mind. It was Friday. That was good. She'd finished most of her homework. Her drawings were ready to take to Mrs. Ramsay, and they were going to the Art Institute Saturday afternoon, definitely. Mrs. Ramsay had called. So what then? Carrie flopped over and stared at the ceiling. The dances, of course.

Friday was the last day she could sign up. She had to do it. Her mother's check had been sitting in her purse for weeks.

It was still dark. Carrie sat up and looked out the window at the pale bulk of the house from which Mrs. Padmore's soul had flown. She imagined how it had looked, sailing out the attic window like an empty white nightgown heading higher in the sky.

She imagined escaping out her window now toward the thin strip of graying sky along the horizon, passing over Sylvester, over the Northpoint Club, the golf course, the gas stations beside the expressway, and then over the expressway itself—on and on. Until she reached what? That would be the problem, of course. Where to go.

Carrie got up and switched on a light. Then she padded to the door of Moira's room. The house was cold. Moira was curled in her blankets. Carrie tiptoed to the bed and touched her sister gently. "Moira?"

Moira rolled over, opened her eyes, and looked at Carrie blindly. "What? Didn't I hear it go off? What time is it?" She began groping for the clock.

"No. It's early. It hasn't rung. But, Moira, I have to ask you something."

Moira groaned and sank back on her pillow. "I have to, Moira, I'm sorry."

"It's okay."

"Do I have to go?"

"What are you talking about?"

"The dances."

"God, Carrie, it's six o'clock!"

"I know. I'm sorry, but what do you think?"

Moira heaved herself up on her pillow and yawned. Then she leaned over and turned on her lamp. "What's wrong?"

"I need to know if I *have* to go."

"It's really worrying you, isn't it?"

Carrie nodded.

"I don't see why. It's no big deal."

"I don't know why either. But, Moira, I really don't want to."

"Carrie, *everybody* goes to those dances in eighth grade. Do you want to be weird?"

"You know me, Moira. You know how I am."

"All you do is go to the club. Mrs. Mitchell plays records and teaches you some old stuff, and then everybody dances any way they want for the second hour."

Carrie shivered. Moira handed her the quilt. "Here. You look like you're freezing."

Carrie wrapped the quilt around her shoulders, but she couldn't stop shaking. Even her voice shook. "I can't go to a dance," she said.

"Listen, Care." Moira began picking at the hem of the sheet without looking up, as if she were embarrassed. "I've been thinking about this for a while. You know how last summer you were always talking about going down to the pond like we used to? About the fish and all?"

Carrie nodded.

"Well, I'm too old for that, Carrie. I've been too old for years now. But, Carrie, the thing is—so are you. I don't know how to say it. I know you think Mother's being unreasonable, but she's not. It's time. You can't go on and on being a little kid, Carrie—there's something queer about that!''

Carrie pulled the quilt tighter around her. Her teeth were chattering, and she had to try to keep her voice steady. ''You don't care about the goldfish?'' she said.

''I *used* to! That used to be fun when we were little girls, but we aren't little girls now. You're thirteen years old, for God's sake!''

Carrie bent her head and studied the stitching on the quilt.

''Are you mad?'' Moira asked.

''No.''

''I wasn't trying to hurt your feelings. But you ought to think about it, Carrie.''

''I think about it.''

''Okay.''

Carrie unwound herself from the quilt and spread it neatly back on the bed. ''I'll call you when it's seven,'' she said.

Eighth hour, Carrie got an excuse from study hall and went down to Mr. Adderley's office. His secretary was typing midterm reports. On her desk was a crepe-paper turkey, the kind that opens like an accordion and hooks together. She had a pumpkin at Halloween, a heart for Valentine's Day—whatever was seasonal.

''I came to sign up for the dances,'' Carrie said when there was a pause in the typing. ''I have a check.''

Mr. Adderley's secretary swiveled her chair around to the files behind her. "You really waited for the deadline, didn't you? Let's see. I've already put the folder away." She rummaged in the bottom drawer and pulled out a manila folder. "Here. You just add your name to the list."

Carrie signed. Mr. Adderley's secretary smiled. "I can't believe how you kids grow up. Every year when I do these sign-ups I think, Well, there goes another bunch. Next thing I know they'll have graduated. Now give me your check and I'll make out a receipt."

Carrie handed over the check and stared at the crepe-paper turkey while Mr. Adderley's secretary wrote the receipt. In a way the turkey looked like Mr. Adderley's secretary—especially the neck. Carrie almost laughed. She felt light-headed.

Mr. Adderley's secretary waved the receipt. "All signed up," she said.

And then, quite suddenly, it happened again. Something in Carrie's head slipped sideways. The kaleidoscope pieces appeared, clattered, slid. Her head grew lighter. A roaring began, as if a train had jumped the track and were rushing down the hall outside the door. Carrie gripped the edge of the desk. She was swimming through noise. She closed her eyes.

"Carrie?" From far away Mr. Adderley's secretary was calling. "Carrie, are you sick?"

Her voice swam, rose higher, and dissolved in the roaring—a record running too fast. Pieces of glass. A turkey gobbling. And out of the chaos then, all at once, a bit of land—a sunny, quiet rock—floated up, bobbed, and disappeared.

Carrie breathed in. The voice began to reassemble itself. Slowly there were words. The roaring grew softer. Carrie opened her eyes.

"Are you all right?" Mr. Adderley's secretary leaned across the desk and put her hand on Carrie's.

"I'm okay. It was just a dizzy spell. I didn't eat lunch."

"You shouldn't skip lunch. You go right home now and eat something. I'll excuse you."

But instead Carrie went back to study hall. If she went home early she'd have to explain, and it was a lie about lunch. She opened her math book and looked at the problems for Monday.

Lots of people had dizzy spells, she thought. People fainted. Once, in history class, Beth Cromwell had fallen right over, and afterward everybody said it was cramps. But this wasn't that, of course. This was something else. It scared her.

◦8◦

But as it had the first time, the whole experience faded quickly and began to seem unreal. By the time she set out for Chicago with Mrs. Ramsay on Saturday afternoon, Carrie had almost forgotten it.

The Art Institute was jammed. A group of schoolchildren

was being herded through the front door, and, inside, people milled in the lobby. "Saturday," said Mrs. Ramsay, "is the worst day to come." She had Noah and Saskia firmly in hand. "I'm afraid we'll have to spend a certain amount of time looking at armor."

"That's okay," Carrie said. "I like armor."

"Yes, but I want you to have plenty of time for the show. I imagine you've seen the armor a thousand times. It doesn't change." All of this she more or less shouted over her shoulder as they wove through the crowd.

Carrie dodged after her. She was happy to be there. She loved the museum with its great pale rooms and quiet light—gray-blue and still like winter light.

Mrs. Ramsay had reached the ticket booth and was paying. Noah dashed ahead and began to climb the marble staircase to the second floor. "You go ahead to the exhibit," Mrs. Ramsay said. "I'll take them to the armor for a while."

"I don't mind coming along. Really."

"No. I feel guilty. It's not your fault I couldn't find a sitter. I want you to look at what those artists did with line, Carrie. You'll love it. More than that, you'll understand it."

Noah began shouting from the top of the staircase.

Carrie climbed to the second floor with them and then left to follow signs to the Art Nouveau exhibit. She had to pay again at the entrance, so she didn't have enough left to buy a catalogue. But it didn't matter. It seemed to her that nothing mattered but the pure pleasure of being there.

She moved slowly along the wall from picture to picture, trying to keep some distance between herself and the people ahead. She disliked having to duck and dodge around someone else in order to see. Behind her, two art students followed with open notebooks and pencils. They made notes, spoke in whispers.

Carrie looked obediently at line. She didn't know what it was she was supposed to see. She didn't understand. She passed half a dozen small pictures slowly, trying to look with Mrs. Ramsay's eyes, and stopped before a painting of three women on a ladder by a Frenchman named Maurice Denis. It reminded her of the illustrations in her old *Blue Fairy Book*—fussy and elaborate. She didn't like it.

The art students passed behind her after stopping, one on either side, to survey the painting. "You can see the Japanese influence," one murmured to the other.

"Yes, but facile."

Meaning what? Carrie wondered. What was facile? She felt afloat in her own ignorance. And then suddenly she saw what Mrs. Ramsay meant. The line.

The picture was, in fact, almost nothing else—line that became twisting, curving tendrils, meandering, snake-like, up and down and across the canvas. The painting was a jungle of curving lines, cut across by the straight diagonals of the ladder. The foliage and the figures of the women were really simply studies in curve. Carrie stood dumbfounded before the picture. Now that she had seen what was there, she could not imagine seeing it otherwise.

After a while she moved on past two Gauguins, then past

a series of woodcuts. The sinuous line was everywhere, snaking and twisting across the pictures, flowing into their frames, leading her from one to another as if she were following a magic thread.

She went into the next room and the next, through galleries where the line spilled itself onto the carved arms of chairs, climbed across mirrors, and twisted itself into stained-glass panels. There was a room of posters advertising ordinary things—brands of tobacco, openings of plays, where the line became words. Then it crept, serpentine, into the figures on the posters. Like a wild grapevine it crawled over and around and through every object on display.

Carrie was mesmerized. Sometimes the line reminded her of water running quickly in shallow curves in the gutters in the spring. Other times it was gentle and meandering in a lazy, slow, deep-summer way.

She moved as if sleepwalking. The light, the room, the voices of people in the room were vague, a distant distraction of crickets. She had forgotten the cool, precise light and the high pale rooms. Her body had become another curving shape, bending and soft. Vaguely she wondered what it was she was feeling, but she kept moving on.

At first, when she stopped before the drawing, she didn't really see it. She looked with eyes grown drowsy and distracted. Then slowly she saw and abruptly stopped still.

It was a picture of a pond. A strange sort of water lily bloomed on the surface, and leaning over the bank was a woman with trailing hair. Carrie knew how the water would smell—warm and stagnant with rotting leaves. And under the greenish surface there would be flashes of gold where fish were hiding. She smiled softly. If the woman would whistle—and then she caught her breath. She saw in horror that the woman was holding a man's head.

Just the head. There was no body. His hair was a dozen twisting snakes and from the stump of his neck a long liquid curve fell back into the water.

"Aubrey Beardsley," Mrs. Ramsay said. She was standing—for how long had she been there?—beside Carrie. She put a hand on Carrie's shoulder. "What do you think of it?"

"What *is* it?" Carrie whispered.

"Salome with the head of John the Baptist."

"From the Bible?"

"Well, with Beardsley's interpretation."

Carrie turned to see whether Mrs. Ramsay was shocked, but she didn't seem to be. She was slitting her gray eyes the way she did when she looked at a student's drawing, treating it like any other picture. "You know the story?"

Carrie shook her head.

"No? I'm surprised. Well, you see, Salome wanted John the Baptist, but he wouldn't have her. He ignored her. And then she wanted revenge. You've heard of the Dance of the Seven Veils."

Carrie nodded.

"I always imagine that dance as very slow and undulating—Salome moving like a snake. Anyway, she danced in her veils for the King. He was mesmerized. He promised her anything if she would be his. She asked for the head of

John the Baptist. It was brought to her on a tray.''

"But how could he do that?'' Carrie said. "The King, I mean. Because of a dance?''

"Well, darling, sex is powerful magic sometimes.''

Carrie looked down at the toes of her boots and at the solid marble floor beneath them. She wished Mrs. Ramsay hadn't said that. "I guess so,'' she replied.

"Have you liked the exhibit?'' said Mrs. Ramsay.

Carrie nodded, not looking directly at her.

"I came through it quickly because the children are waiting downstairs, but it's overpowering, isn't it? I think it's the cumulative effect of all that sensuality, that sensuous line. It overwhelms me.''

"It's like a grapevine,'' Carrie said flatly.

"Well, of course, but much more. Didn't you feel it?''

Carrie looked out past the pictures toward the bright pale room beyond, where there was a display of eighteenth-century furniture. She wanted to be there. She wanted to get away from the line. "We better go find the twins,'' she said.

On the train ride home Noah and Saskia whined. They started almost the minute the train pulled out of Union Station tunnel, and they kept it up. Mrs. Ramsay talked above them, telling Carrie that she'd mailed off her drawings, telling her something more about Beardsley. Carrie half listened. Her head ached. She felt as she often had years ago when she and Moira had come out of an afternoon matinee into the bright sunshine of a Saturday afternoon. She hated that feeling—headachy and somehow guilty. Those after-noons they'd run all the way home, kicking stones, trying to lose the feeling.

Mrs. Ramsay's old Plymouth was parked at the North-point station. She offered Carrie a ride. "No, thanks. I think I'll walk," Carrie said. "It's nice out."

Mrs. Ramsay opened the door for the twins. "Sorry about them," she said. "Next time I'll find a sitter."

Carrie watched the rusty old car climb the hill from the station before she started home. Then she buttoned her coat and began to run, head down against the wind. It felt good to be running.

∘9∘

Carrie floated through Sunday. Occasionally she thought of the exhibit and of how she'd felt there. Then, very delib-erately, she'd think of something else. Later she hardly remembered Sunday at all, and she supposed that was strange.

On Monday Mr. Adderley opened assembly by warning them that, although it was Thanksgiving week, there were still three school days left and he expected students to act accordingly. He said the same thing every year, but, Carrie thought, he must know it was useless. The three days before vacation were for her, as they were for everyone else at Sylvester, wasted time. Classes were noisy. By Wednesday afternoon the study halls were electric and few people made even a pretense of working.

Carrie drifted through these days. When she looked back at it, she realized that it was then, early in Thanksgiving week, that the trouble had begun to grow too large for her. But she hadn't recognized it for what it was. She had thought she was like the rest of them, preoccupied with drifting toward a vacation.

She began to know it was something else that Wednesday afternoon. Halfway through seventh-hour study hall she gave up trying to work and got a pass to go down to the art room.

Mrs. Ramsay, in a color-encrusted smock, was putting away paint jars. The long tables were scattered with wet paintings from the last class—clumsy still lifes of bittersweet and apples. "Do you want some help cleaning up?" Carrie asked. "I gave up trying to study."

"I'd love it. There are twenty or thirty brushes in the sink, if you don't mind."

"The kids didn't clean them?"

"No. It's the seventh graders. They were so wild today I let them paint till the bell."

Carrie went to work on the brushes. "The whole school's wild."

"Always before a vacation."

The room smelled of damp paper and poster paint. Outside, snow spit fretfully against the windows. Overhead lights glared. The radiators hissed. Mrs. Ramsay whistled tunelessly, stacking jars. And from far down the hall came the voices of the high-school glee club, already practicing Christmas music.

Carrie was content. She held the brushes under the running water, felt the water run over her hand and splash into the sink. Things seemed better to her than they had in days. "I liked the Denis," she said impulsively, and then, "I didn't get it right away. But suddenly I did. It was there that I saw what you meant about line."

Carrie was pleased. It was the first time she'd been able to think easily about the exhibit. She thought about it now without discomfort. They had been, after all, only pictures.

"I think it's lucky I had to go see the armor," Mrs. Ramsay said. "That way you discovered it alone. I'd probably have explained too much."

"It took a while."

"Well, those pictures seem so fussy and old-fashioned at first."

"Like old storybook illustrations."

"Yes. Some of them. Until you see what they're up to, how they're making the line itself expressive."

Carrie nodded, swished the brushes under the water. Mrs. Ramsay began chipping caked paint from around the mouth of a jar. "But," she said, "you didn't like the Beardsley."

"No." Carrie could feel herself stiffen.

"Or was it what I said that you didn't like?"

Carrie looked down at the brush in her hand. "I don't know."

"I probably made it sound mysterious. All I meant to do

was explain why Herod gave Salome the head of the prophet.''

"That's okay," Carrie said in a tight voice. "It doesn't make any difference." And she bent to work on a brush, flattening the bristles against her palm under the water. She wanted the conversation to end there. It was tearing a hole in the peacefulness of the room. She could feel herself beginning to breathe more quickly.

"What doesn't make any difference?"

"What you said."

"About sex being powerful? But, honey, it is. It makes an enormous difference. That's just true."

Carrie swallowed. She watched the brush in her hand run red into the sink. She watched red run into the crevices and wrinkles of her palm. She tried to hear what the glee club was singing. She tried to hear the snow.

"Carrie?"

"I know."

"Well, then?"

And suddenly, without knowing she would, Carrie screamed. She turned blindly away from the sink, letting the handful of brushes drop. "Carrie, what happened?" Mrs. Ramsay's voice came from a great distance.

Her head was whirling. The kaleidoscope pieces began to slide wildly, growing huge, like shelves of rock slipping along a fault. The roaring drowned the choir, the running water, Mrs. Ramsay's voice. Carrie desperately wanted her feet to move. With a vast, wrenching effort she ran.

She found she was running down Hartman. Her old duffel coat flapped from her shoulders like broken wings. She couldn't remember going to the locker to get it or leaving school or anything at all until that moment. Wind-whipped snow stung her face. Her feet were icy. She watched them running, slapping down on the wet pavement like objects unattached. Her breath came painfully. Her chest was full of claws. I am going crazy, she thought, and the thought became a scream. Out loud? She couldn't tell. The noise in her chest and the wind and the slap of her feet and the great roaring inside her head deafened her.

The entrance to the Northpoint Clinic swam up ahead. Carrie shoved through the door and ran for the stairs. Her father's waiting room was full of people. Miss Phelps looked up, then jumped up. "I have to see my father," Carrie gasped. "I can't wait."

Then somehow she was in one of her father's examining rooms. Her father was in the doorway and, behind him, Miss Phelps. "What have you done to yourself?" He was staring at her hand.

Carrie looked down stupidly. Her left hand was caked with red. "Oh," she said. "Paint."

"Paint!" Miss Phelps began laughing shrilly. "Oh, I thought she was cut! Oh, thank goodness!"

Carrie's father closed the door abruptly, almost rudely, on Miss Phelps. He seemed suddenly enormous to Carrie and like someone else in his long white coat. "What happened, honey?"

Carrie opened her mouth, but instead of speaking, she doubled over as if someone had struck her and knocked out her wind. She whispered, "I can't help it. I can't stop it any more."

She stared at the floor, watching the patterns in the tile swim and disappear and swim up again. She felt her father's hand on her head. Gradually she began to breathe more slowly. The tiles held still. She straightened up.

Her father washed her hand clean. He gave her some water to drink and a wet towel for her eyes. Carrie sat limp on the edge of the examining table. She was exhausted. Irrelevantly she noticed that her feet almost touched the table's step. As if he saw the same thing, her father said, "You've grown a lot taller this year."

Carrie nodded.

"You've got something big on your mind."

Again she nodded, and then, in short, frightened sentences, she told him what was happening.

"I wonder whether you're low on iron," he said when she'd finished.

She looked up at him wildly, uncomprehending. Didn't he hear what she was saying?

"Dizziness is pretty common in girls your age."

"I don't think it's like that," Carrie whispered. "I think there's something wrong in my head."

"Oh, no. You're probably a little anemic. That's something we can find out."

Carrie watched him go to a cabinet and take out a syringe. "Daddy, please," she said, but the words sounded jumbled to her. She wasn't sure she'd said them. She sat quiet while he drew a syringe of blood from her arm.

Exactly the color of the dried paint, her own dark blood. She turned her head away. The sight sickened her.

"Now," he said, "we'll send this to the lab and have it tested. And I'll have Miss Phelps call Mother to come get you. You lie down this afternoon. Take it easy."

Inside her head words swarmed, trying to escape into the cool air of the examining room. They buzzed in her throat just behind her tongue, but they were stuck there. The word she needed—"crazy"—fell dead in the dark wet cave of her mouth, and she climbed off the examining table and waited obediently while Miss Phelps called her mother. Then she stood inside the glass doors of the clinic, waiting for her mother's navy blue Lincoln.

The car was warm. The wipers swished rhythmically, wiping snow from the windshield. Her mother's voice rattled like an empty tin can, and Carrie leaned back against the fat padded seat and closed her eyes.

"You should eat more breakfast," her mother said.

"Yes."

"Eggs. Daddy thinks you're anemic."

"Um." Carrie nodded.

"Aunt Beth and Uncle Walter are driving over tomorrow if the roads aren't impossible. Do you mind if I stop a minute at The Pantry on the way home?"

"No," Carrie said. They stopped. When they went on, there was a paper bag on the seat between them.

"Saturday we're having people for cocktails. I was thinking that Friday we'd go into Saks and find you a dress."

"I think I'm going crazy," Carrie said softly, watching the wipers curve across the windshield.

"What?"

"Something's wrong."

"If you'd get to bed earlier and eat a proper breakfast, you wouldn't have these dizzy spells."

"Why don't you listen to what I'm telling you? Why do you keep saying anemic and breakfast?"

"Carrie, look, I have a thousand things to do this weekend. Just don't be silly, okay?"

The wipers swished quietly. Carrie watched them. The car moved and jerked and moved again, and then it stopped and they were home.

"I'll get you some aspirin."

Carrie lay down. She could hear her mother rummaging in the hall closet for aspirin. They kept all the medicine there—cough syrup, half-used bottles of penicillin, tetracycline, sleeping pills. When they'd first moved to Northpoint, it had all been kept in a box on the top shelf because of Duncan. Moira and Carrie were already old enough to know that if you took too much medicine it could kill you, but Duncan was little then.

Carrie closed her eyes and floated. She swallowed the aspirin her mother brought, then curled under her quilt and fell asleep.

Later she heard Moira look in. Later still, her mother came into the room and put a hand on her forehead. She could feel through closed eyelids that her mother was look-

52

ing down at her face. She could imagine the expression, slightly frowning, confused. She'd seen that look for as long as she could remember, times when she was sick, as though it were beyond her mother to understand, out of her own unfailing good health, sickly children.

By six-thirty the house was quiet. Moira and her parents had gone to parties. Sophie brought supper on a tray, and afterward Carrie watched television with Duncan.

"You got flu again or what?" Duncan said.

"I don't know."

"Well, if you think it's flu, keep away from me. I got a hockey tournament this weekend." Then he turned back to the screen. His narrow little face was blue in the blue light.

"Will you get to play?" Carrie asked.

Duncan turned back to her abstractedly. "What?"

"Will you play?"

He shrugged his thin shoulders. "I hope they put me in."

Carrie curled up. The program was terrible.

"You want me to come watch your game?" Carrie said.

"If you want to. Sure."

"When is it?"

"The tournament starts Friday. If we win, it's all weekend."

Carrie nodded and snuggled down. The next program seemed better.

10

Thanksgiving Day. Aunt Beth and Uncle Walter came from Oak Park every year for Thanksgiving dinner. They weren't actually relatives, but Carrie and Moira and Duncan were supposed to call them aunt and uncle as though they were.

Aunt Beth brought pies—a pumpkin and a mince. Carrie's father made whiskey sours, which the adults drank in the living room, sitting on the matching flowered love seats. Duncan watched the Macy parade on television. Moira and Carrie, in dresses and stockings, helped Sophie in the kitchen.

Every year it was the same. This year, too. Aunt Beth and Uncle Walter came at noon. The house smelled wonderful, of roasting turkey. There were chrysanthemums in a crystal vase on the coffee table. There was a great deal of talk about slippery roads, and there were maraschino cherries in the drinks. Carrie tried to notice carefully. She held firmly to each detail, as if she were a mountain climber negotiating the sheer face of the day.

Friday began better. When she woke, she thought it might stay that way. Early sun touched the top of the bare maple outside her window. The room was cold.

She got up and closed the window. There was a thin layer of snow on the ground, not enough to really cover. Somebody had already swept the front walk. As she watched, Duncan came around the side of the house, carrying his hockey stick, with his skates tied over his shoulder. A minute later the Slopers' car slowed down in front. Duncan climbed in the back and the car moved on, sliding a little sideways as it gained speed.

Carrie stood shivering at the window. The tire tracks reminded her of a time long ago, walking with her father in Hyde Park after an early snowfall. They'd left a double set of tracks, a small one and a large one. When they came home, the snow had melted. The tracks were gone.

"Where do footprints go when the snow melts?" Carrie had asked.

"They disappear."

"But where do they *go*?" Everything had to go somewhere in her experience. She could see herself that the snow had not disappeared but had become water on the sidewalk.

"Honey, they just vanish."

"No!" she'd screamed, because her father hadn't understood what she meant. He hadn't seen that the fact that something could vanish entirely was terrifying.

At breakfast her mother reminded her that they were going to Chicago. At noon they took the train.

Carrie sat beside her mother. Moira sat across the aisle, trying to finish *Silas Marner*. It was snowing again. Carrie tried to remember what she had done between breakfast and the train, but she couldn't. She tried to think how she'd gotten there. She was wearing her plaid kilt. She couldn't remember dressing.

"Something simple," her mother was saying. "I don't mean it has to be elaborate, but there isn't a thing in your closet that's suitable."

She's talking about clothes, Carrie thought. A dress for

the dances. This is why we're going to Chicago. She's telling me what we are going to buy.

"A nice bright color," her mother said.

Carrie watched telephone poles slide past the window, falling backward out of sight, chopped down by the passing train.

"Carrie, are you listening?"

Carrie turned. Her mother's face slid into focus, intruding like a loud noise. Carrie concentrated on the two faint vertical lines between her mother's eyebrows. They ran parallel—tiny train tracks—going where?

"And you'll need shoes, too."

Carrie nodded, staring at the lines. If she could follow them into her mother's head, behind her eyes, deep into her mind, what would she see? Who knows? No entry. The tracks stopped short at the bridge of her mother's nose.

"Carrie, you're acting as if you were still asleep."

And then the lines disappeared and were replaced by the back of her mother's head. She is talking to Moira, Carrie thought. Good. With relief Carrie let her concentration slide. Telephone poles again. Trees. Cars at a crossing.

Once in Chicago she'd seen her mother crying, standing on the fire escape outside the kitchen door. Why? She wore a dressing gown. Carrie held a sneaker. She needed to have her mother tie it. She caught the dressing gown between her fingers and patted her mother's leg. She stood on the fire escape and held her mother's leg. But her mother was crying, and she didn't like it. Before Duncan was born.

Before Duncan was born, Carrie had felt him move inside

56

her mother. They had put their heads against her stomach—Moira on one side, Carrie on the other—and waited. Carrie had watched Moira's face for fear she wouldn't know when it happened. And then she had felt the movement, and she had reached for Moira's hand.

Where was Moira's hand now? No hand.

Beyond Morton Grove the snow changed. Thick, fat flakes brushed past the windows of the train like feathers. Carrie watched the flakes descend, spiral up, and fall again, different from leaves but with patterns of movement that reminded her of her drawings. Here it was not one but millions of separate movements. It would take acres of paper to explore the shapes of a snowfall, years of drawing, a whole lifetime to put on paper what she could see through a single train window.

Wind ruffled the flakes and sent them into high, slowly descending curves. Carrie turned away from the curving and stared at her hands in her lap.

"Better gather up," her mother said.

Moira was winding on her muffler. They were in Union Station tunnel. Carrie found her coat on the overhead rack.

They took a taxi from the station. "I hope we can get back home. This is beginning to look like a blizzard," her mother said.

"It would be kind of fun to be stranded," Moira said.

"Not with forty people coming for cocktails tomorrow night."

The taxi turned onto Michigan Avenue at the bridge. Carrie huddled down into her coat and stared at the buildings growing vague behind a curtain of falling snow. She felt peaceful, as if she, too, were withdrawing into the snow.

Saks. Second floor. There were silver Christmas decorations, mothers and daughters everywhere. They had to wait for a fitting room.

Moira and her mother riffled through racks along the wall. Occasionally her mother pulled out a dress and held it toward her, questioning. Then they tunneled through narrow halls, past curtained doorways to a room with hangers and a chair.

"Carrie, try this. It looks just about right to me."

The dress was flowered, rose and lavender. Carrie slipped it over her head. She stood obediently while the back was fastened. "Oh," said the saleswoman, "isn't it perfect?" Then she turned to fasten Moira.

Carrie looked at herself in the mirror. Brightness and shine. The flowers were crumbs flung against the silvery surface.

"What do you think?" Her mother's voice.

Carrie stared. The spots of color shifted, slid, swam across the glass like waterbugs.

"Fine," she said.

"Well, do you *really* like it or are you just saying so?"

"No. It's fine."

The roaring was gentle and far off. The rocks slipped easily along the fault, and the colors swarmed like fish skimming just below the surface of the mirror. Carrie knew that it was beginning again, but this time she was not frightened.

She saw that she could ride it as if it were a current running out. She could go with it. It would carry her gently out beyond the room to wherever it was going. If she let it.

She lifted off the dress, put on her kilt, and waited while Moira tried garment after garment. She saw herself doing this as if she were watching a girl her size whom she recognized from some other place.

"Easy to please," the saleswoman said.

"She really hasn't much interest in clothes."

"Look. Don't you think this one is too high-waisted?"

"That's the way it's cut, dear."

"Moira, please make up your mind. I'd like to catch the four-thirty."

Flies buzzing against a window screen, far off, muffled by falling snow. Falling petals. Petals like feathers. Riding the current. Riding through the streets. Floating on the train until the train reached home.

In the front hall Duncan. Duncan waiting with shining eyes. "We made the semis! We're in the semifinals, Care!"

"Oh. Duncan." His face floated toward her, forming itself.

"Now you can come tomorrow to watch us like you said. I can save places for everyone halfway up where you can really see. Some kids don't save places and their families get stuck behind a post or something."

Carrie put an arm around his shoulders. His shoulder blades felt fragile as bird bones. She closed her eyes and hugged him and felt him warming her. Then he squirmed out of her embrace. "So you're all coming, right?"

Moira was piling packages on the hall table. "When is it, Dunc?"

"Five o'clock."

"Oh, Duncan, I can't then. I have choir rehearsal four to six." Moira began unwinding her scarf.

"And Daddy and I are having a party. I don't see how we can do it, either." Their mother looked at him thoughtfully, smoothed his hair with a gloved hand. "I'm sorry. If I'd had some idea this was coming up—"

"You can't tell ahead if you're going to be in the semifinals," Duncan said. "Carrie, you can come."

"I told you I would."

"I can save *one* place easily."

Carrie closed her eyes and pushed hard against the current. She needed to be all right for Duncan.

"What's wrong?" he asked.

She made her eyes focus on his face. "Nothing."

"Are you still sick? You don't have to come."

"I'm coming."

She would go. The game was a tiny light a whole day away. She would think about it, keep watching it, and by concentrating hard on the spark of light, she would navigate the hours until bed.

11

On Saturday it was still snowing. The path to the garage had disappeared overnight, and the bushes around the house bent low under the weight of drifts.

Sophie greeted Carrie at lunchtime, grumbling. "Peanut butter, that's it today. I got eight kinds of hors d'oeuvres to fix."

Her mother was making lists, checking things off. "I hope Wilson can make it through the snow."

Wilson, the bartender.

"We'll be all right if the snow stops."

Carrie imagined the snow stopping, pausing in midair and refusing to fall. A cloud of snow hanging above the roof. Stubborn.

Overhead a thump.

Her mother looked up at the dining room ceiling. "Someday he's going to knock down the plaster."

Duncan's weights. Duncan's game. Carrie made herself think about the game.

During the afternoon the snow stopped. There were glasses washed and lined up in the kitchen. Bottles. Sophie vacuumed the living room. Flowers arrived.

"Remember, Care, you got to get there *before* five. It starts at five."

"Yes."

"If you want you can go with the Slopers. They're driving. Only we go pretty early."

"I'll walk."

It was not much more than half a mile to the rink. The sky was already blue with twilight when Carrie set out. Wind had begun drifting the snow again, and Carrie bent against the wind, huddling in her coat.

As she passed the corner where, weekdays, she would turn toward Sylvester, the streetlights came on. Farther along, beyond the Standard station, a car was spinning its wheels. It spun, stopped, spun again, making a hopeless whining sound. At the next corner she turned east.

The light from the streetlamps left yellow smudges on the snow. Somewhere a dog was barking. A car passed, going slowly, leaving tiny staccato clouds of exhaust behind. Carrie dug her hands into the pockets of her coat and breathed in the cold, exhaling vapor. Her boots flapped rhythmically.

Now she was making tracks where no one had been before. The snow stretched ahead of her, unmarked as a fresh sheet of drawing paper, no print or tire mark or fallen branch for as far as she could see. Blue snow, yellow spots of streetlight, and wind lifting flurries off the drifts along the road.

At the back of her mind there was something floating. It was both there and ahead of her, just beyond. Something warm. She could see it even as she watched her boots moving. She could see moss on rocks above green water. She could see fish swimming in gold and orange schools.

This was where the current wanted to take her. Suddenly Carrie knew that if she called them, the fish would carry her. She wanted to call them. She wanted to be lapped with warm water.

But there was Duncan. She thought of Duncan and of her boots flapping. She tried to think. Yet the rocky island grew larger. She was approaching. She was riding the current, carried by the fish. She could see rocks where white birds were roosting. They fluttered up and settled back as if borne on updrafts of wind.

Then there was a building and the street stopped.

Carrie looked around her, bewildered. The island was gone. She recognized the ramshackle building as one that bordered the Northpoint landfill. The landfill abutted the expressway. She was nowhere near the rink. She was blocks beyond streetlights and houses. She was at the farthest edge of town. Carrie stood still and tried to think how she had come there. Somewhere she had made a wrong turn.

Wind whipped across the landfill. Blowing snow skittered like mouse feet. Carrie hunched into her coat and turned her back to the wind. How had she done this?

As she stood there, headlights appeared from behind the building. A pickup truck pulled out into the street and started forward, then stopped.

"Need a ride?" A man leaned out the window toward her.

Carrie started to refuse, then nodded. He opened the door. "Pretty cold night to be way out here."

"I got lost," Carrie said.

"Where you headed?"

"I was on my way to the ice rink to watch my brother's game."

"Well, you're a long way from there."

"Is it past five?"

"Past five! It's past seven!"

"Then I missed it."

The man looked at her curiously. He put the truck into gear. "How about I take you home then? Where do you live?"

Carrie told him.

"You'd have had a long walk."

"I thought I was going the right way. I wanted to see the game."

"You're lucky you didn't freeze."

The truck bounced and slid up the street from the landfill. They began to pass houses Carrie didn't remember seeing before. Stores. A gas station. Yet she must have passed them earlier. "You're sure it's after seven?"

"Ten after."

Where had she been for two and a half hours? Carrie tried to think and knew she didn't know. Walking. She held her breath and shivered.

"Still cold?"

Carrie shook her head. For two and a half hours she had been nowhere, drifting toward an island that was more real than the streets. Carrie shivered and then couldn't stop trembling.

"I got the heater up as high as it will go."

"There's something wrong."

"You're cold clear through."

"No. I am going crazy. I don't know where I've been."

The man glanced sideways. "Your mom and dad at home?"

Carrie didn't answer. The roaring had begun. But this time she recognized that it was the noise that water made, washing far off against the rocks. Her head floated lightly. Colors swam and sank. She closed her eyes and rested against the back of the seat.

<h2 style="text-align:center">◦ 12 ◦</h2>

"This it here? With all the lights?"

Carrie heard the man's voice coming over miles of water. She was in a truck. She turned to him, questioning.

"This your house?"

The house swam up ahead. Carrie pulled herself back slowly, hand over hand, until the house and the man and the truck came clear.

"Yes," she said, "this is it."

"Looks like a party."

"Yes." She had forgotten.

"You go right in now and get yourself warmed up. Take care."

Carrie climbed out and slammed the door. The house was loud with light. She went around back and let herself in the kitchen door. Sophie was bending into the oven. "Where have you been?"

Carrie leaned in the kitchen doorway, collecting words. They swarmed in her head like insects. Somewhere there were the right ones for answering Sophie. She sorted among them with terrible effort.

"Well, where?"

"I couldn't find the rink."

"You couldn't find the rink since four-thirty?"

The edge of the island. Not now. First Sophie.

"Duncan was about brokenhearted no one showed up. You should have kept your promise to him, Carrie."

An upswarming bright cloud of words to choose from. Duncan. "Where is Duncan?"

"Let him be for now."

Carrie leaned heavily against the doorjamb. The kitchen swam sideways, righted itself. She thought of crossing the floor, going up the back stairs. She would lose her way. She had forgotten the path.

A crash. Sophie clattered a cookie sheet onto the kitchen table. Wilson came through the swinging door from the dining room with an empty drink tray. After him a burst of talk and laughter opened like a red parasol. Shut.

Pick up words. Lay them straight. Make the ends touch. "Where is Duncan?" With his light bird bones and his face like a match flame.

Sophie was arranging cheese puffs. "Sophie?"

Black silky back. Edge of an apron. "Sophie?"

"I said let him be a while. Later you can talk. You want

66

to be useful right now? Pass these for me. My leg's real bad tonight."

Bad leg. Thick in an elastic stocking.

"Please. While they're hot."

Carrie moved from the door. The kitchen tipped sideways. She was walking like a fly clinging to a wall. "For Lord's sake, Carrie, hold that tray straight! You're going to have the whole bunch of them on the floor."

The swinging door. Push—swings out.

Suddenly bright umbrellas of noise exploding. Colors sliding. Drifts of brightness blowing across the carpet. Far away the water is lapping the cliffs.

Careful. Don't remember. Walk between the people. Hold the tray straight. Stop. Go on.

Pass between ferns in a deep fern thicket. There are birds in the branches screaming like parrots.

Hold the tray straight. Edge between. Stop for Mrs. Palmer. Now Mrs. Stanley. Mrs. Stanley has a snake on the back of her dress. No. A pattern. Keep it straight.

Where is Duncan? Sitting and waiting, holding his broken-bird-heart in his hand. You should have kept your word. I couldn't. Where is it? Where did I leave it? I took the wrong turn.

The man in the truck. Think. Where was it? Where were you? Shaking like a wet dog. I was cold. No. I was going crazy. I am shaking loose my brains. They are falling on the rug.

Glass voices breaking. Razor voices falling. Don't go barefoot here. There are pieces on the rug.

Face. Mother.

"Carrie dear, you remember Georgina Findley?"

Careful. Hand out. Remember Mrs. Findley.

"I'd never have known her! She's grown like a weed."

Dandelion. Crab grass. Dig them out and kill them. Tracks between the eyes going nowhere.

"Do you remember Alice, Carrie? She used to sit for you when you were small."

Alice. No. Find some words.

"Carrie, Mrs. Findley asked you a question."

Put them together. Make them touch at the ends. "No. I don't remember Alice."

"Alice is older, of course. She has a baby. Doesn't seem to take any time and they're grown."

"Carrie liked Alice."

"Doesn't take any time at all. Braces and bicycles and, before you know it, babies. I'll bet this is your year for the junior dances, Carrie."

Move. This is hard. The words keep sliding.

"Carrie dear, will you answer Mrs. Findley?"

Better move. Find the island. Whistle for the fish.

"And then proms and, next, weddings."

Where is it? The island.

"Carrie's first dance is next week. Of course, we've been through it all before with Moira."

Whistle then. Hurry. Call the fish. They can find you.

"Carrie?"

Softly. Hurry. Whistle for the fish.

"Carrie, for Heaven's sake, what *are* you doing?"

Mrs. Findley's face like a question on a razor. Mother's face like breaking glass. Run. You are drowning in the sharp bright water. Scratching at your eyes. Howling in your ears. The fish can't hear in the loud laughing water. Waves break like mirrors. Teeth in the water. Parrots screaming. Claws in your arm.

No. Run up the stairs. Look for the island. Get to the island before they carry you away.

Upstairs. Hall. Find the hall closet. Find the place where the medicine lives. Bathroom. Lock it. White tile. Bottle. Inside the bottle the island is floating.

Open the bottle. You are going crazy. Float out fast beyond the noise and the faces. Float like Mrs. Padmore. Float across the golf course, cross the expressway toward the tip of the island.

Press and twist. Keep out of reach of children. Blue and orange. Chewy like jujubes. Bitter. Sandy. Take a glass of water. Swallow. Have another. Have a handful. Like peas.

Strange how long it takes to swallow a handful. Longer than peanuts. Gritty like sand. Swallow. Drink water. You are almost there.

The tip of the island swims up into sunlight. The fish flash, shining gold and orange, with translucent tails and glittering sides.

Swim in the air. Fly in the water. Cheek against the smooth, cold white tile floor.

• 13 •

A bright light. Her throat hurt. Something there. Carrie raised her arms slowly and felt for her throat. A tube taped to her cheek.

She opened her eyes. The light was directly above her. The tube came out her nose.

She knew at once she was in a hospital, that the tube in her hand ran from her nose down into her throat and that her stomach had been pumped. She closed her eyes and felt her body sinking down and down. She slept again.

Later she saw a face above hers. Unfamiliar. Later still, her father looking down at her, his head floating like a pale balloon above his white coat.

Each time she woke after that it was the same: the light insisting against her eyelids, the soreness, and sometimes a face. She saw that there was a tube in her arm as well, and a glass bottle upended on a rack over her into which it ran.

She dreamed she was floating above the bed, attached to the earth by flexible tubes. She dreamed she was rolling through narrow halls where noises bloomed suddenly and faded. When she woke, the light was gone.

Again and again she surfaced, felt nothing, slid. Then, again, voices. Then, again, nothing. Over and over. How many times?

Awake, she was troubled. There was something to remember. Carts rattled in the corridor. Voices. There was something she needed to remember.

She woke once to find the soreness in her throat had

disappeared. The tube was gone. A nurse sat in a chair beside the window. Later she saw her father. He bent close to her face. "Awake?" Her tongue would not make the effort to answer. Was this her father's hospital? Was this where he worked?

Sometimes when she woke, the room was dim. At other times sunlight lay in stripes across the bed. Days. How many? She couldn't think. The troubling picked at the edge of her mind. What was it? And then she remembered.

Square white tiles floated up, joined, made a bathroom floor. I tried to kill myself. There it was. Stark as white tile.

Carrie turned her head. The nurse was sitting there, crocheting, enormously fat. Her legs were like huge sausages stuffed into her white stockings. Her shoes were untied.

Carrie studied her sausage fingers twining pink thread, turning it into a pink snake. The crochet hook flashed up and down, catching sunlight. The pink snake curled in the woman's lap. Then the woman looked up. "Well," she said, "waking up?"

Carrie nodded slowly.

"How about some water? I'll bet your throat's dry." She propped Carrie's head and held a bent glass straw to her lips. Close up she smelled of Listerine.

"What day is it?" Carrie said, speaking slowly, as if it had been years since she'd used her voice.

"It's Wednesday."

Which Wednesday? Carrie lay back and was ashamed to ask. The reason she was lying in this hospital overwhelmed her.

"That better?"

"Yes."

The nurse plumped her pillow and straightened the top sheet.

"My arm tube's gone."

"Just a little while ago."

"Does that mean I'm recovered?"

The nurse looked uncomfortable with the question. "That's for Doctor to say."

Doctor. Was that her father or someone else? Carrie closed her eyes and watched spots of color swim under her lids. She didn't want to ask that or anything else for a while. Not yet.

The next time she woke, the room was dark or nearly so. The lamp beside her bed had been turned toward the wall. In the chair by the window a nurse sat dozing. She was a different one, red-haired and younger. Was there always a nurse in the room? Like a guard? Yes, of course. They were guarding her.

Carrie rested her cheek on the pillow and stared at the wall. In the corridor outside there was a rustle; a nurse passed quickly. They were guarding her because she had tried to kill herself. She had tried to kill herself because she was crazy. It was all as simple as the white square tiles that fitted corner to corner and side to side, stretching on beyond her cheek to a vanishing point.

In the morning there was a vase of white carnations beside the bed, and Mrs. Hodges, the fat one, in the chair by the window. "You got a nice bouquet this morning," she said. "Do you want to see the card?"

Carrie opened the little florist's envelope. The flowers were from Mrs. Ramsay. "She's a friend?" Mrs. Hodges asked.

"Yes, and my art teacher."

"That's real nice of her, isn't it? Personally I think carnations are a real nice choice for hospitals. Roses are pretty but the odor gets heavy in a room. Some of the patients I special get nothing but, and I always think it's a mistake. The odor."

Carrie held the card between her thumb and forefinger and read it again. "Love, Mrs. Ramsay" was all it said, but it made her want to cry.

"Let's get your face washed before breakfast," Mrs. Hodges said. Carrie let her wash it. Then she let her hair be brushed while Mrs. Hodges told her about her daughter, Avis, who had a wonderful job in San Diego.

When Mrs. Hodges went for the breakfast tray, Carrie tried standing beside the bed. Her legs shook as if she had been sick for a very long time, and the effort of climbing back into bed exhausted her.

Breakfast was oatmeal. While Carrie ate, Mrs. Hodges talked about Avis's new yellow Charger. It had been a good buy and, of course, cars lasted in California where the weather was better. Carrie nodded and watched the thin bluish milk slowly fill a channel she had made in the cereal. The old oatmeal and mashed potato game that she and

Moira had begun playing when they were babies.

Moira would be hating all this. From every point of view it would upset her. And it would be something she could never understand. It was a rule broken. It was pushing to the edge and beyond the edge. She could imagine Moira's face, withdrawn and bewildered. There would be a time—any time now—when she would have to begin explaining, and she had nothing to say. Carrie settled back on the pillows and let herself drift.

In the morning her mother came. The moment she woke, Carrie knew that it was only a matter of time before that happened. Her father had been there again the night before while she slept. Her mother would be coming.

The room was too warm. Breakfast was oatmeal again. Again Mrs. Hodges washed her face in the stainless-steel bowl. And then, before her hair was brushed, her mother walked in.

She was wearing her black mink coat as if coming to the hospital were some kind of special occasion. She bent and kissed Carrie's forehead, and Carrie could smell her perfume.

Mrs. Hodges made a great flurry of getting up and offering the chair and finding a hanger for the fur coat. "Mink is my favorite. I always say there's lots of nice fur, but give me mink. Not that anyone ever has!" She laughed and winked at Carrie for no reason Carrie could understand. Then she bustled around, gathering up her crocheting. "I'll leave you two alone. If you want me I'll be down at the nurses' station." Carrie's mother smiled and thanked her with the special sort of charm she used for the people she employed.

"Those are lovely carnations," she said after Mrs. Hodges left.

"Mrs. Ramsay sent them."

"Oh? I wonder how she knew you were in the hospital."

"Doesn't everyone?"

This seemed to startle her mother. "Why, no. Your father and I have tried rather hard to keep it quiet."

"What for?"

"Well, it's nobody's business, dear."

"People must know I'm absent from school. Moira would have to give an excuse."

"Just that you're not feeling well."

"That's what you're saying? Like I had a cold?"

"Well, you aren't feeling well."

"But it's not like a cold. You know what happened. I tried to kill myself."

Her mother turned and walked to the window. "Oh, Carrie, I think it was more that you got mixed up, wasn't it? Thought you were taking an aspirin or two? That's what I think."

"It wasn't like that at all," Carrie said softly. "I kept trying to tell all of you."

Her mother leaned against the windowsill, looking out. "I heard on the radio coming over that we're going to get another two or three inches. I don't remember so much snow before Christmas for years."

"I took a whole bottle of pills," Carrie said.

"Duncan got a ninety-eight on his spelling test yesterday. I was so relieved. I think he's finally learning something."

"I took handfuls."

"I meant to bring you a bed jacket. Remember the one with the blue flowers we bought at Saks years ago?"

"I took them because I couldn't help myself any longer."

Her mother turned to face her. Her hands were shaking, pressed against the windowsill. "Carrie, I won't accept what you're saying."

"Why not? I'm telling you the truth."

"You're telling me what you *think* is the truth! Your father, who is a doctor, after all, says he thinks your anemic condition made you especially susceptible to whatever it was. That's all."

"No!" Carrie screamed it, threw the word at her mother like acid. The room tilted wildly. Carrie clung to the bed to keep herself from sliding. The lamp upended. The carnations dissolved and fell in white flakes into the air. "No!"

Mrs. Hodges was there, holding her firmly. Her mother was in the doorway. Then she was gone. Carrie lay rigid, waiting for the room to stop wheeling. "Now then. Now then," Mrs. Hodges repeated like a chant while she held Carrie's arms.

A little later they gave her a shot. Carrie knew it was to make her sleep again. Fine. She wanted to sleep. She smiled, thinking how hard they'd worked to wake her, and now they were putting her to sleep.

She was a doll. Helpless. If they wanted to stand her on

her head they could do that, or leave her in the rain. Wake her. Put her to sleep. Wash her. Brush her hair. Fine, if they wanted to.

And then, for the first time since she had been in the hospital, she saw the island. Suddenly it was there. There had been no approaching it, no journey at all. It appeared behind her eyelids, rocking in the water as gentle as a lullaby. She rested against it, like a dozing baby, and let it rock her softly to sleep.

◦ 14 ◦

The trouble was, they wouldn't let her stay there. He wouldn't. After the first few days, whenever she woke, he was sitting there in Mrs. Hodges's chair, or so it seemed to Carrie. He insisted that she talk to him.

He was so tall that his long legs jackknifed when he sat. His hair looked as if he ran his fingers through it endlessly, and he smoked. He smoked all the time. The first time Carrie saw him, it was his long legs she noticed, and then the ashtray beside him on the arm of the chair. The ashtray was overflowing, as if he had been waiting a long time for her to wake up.

"Who are you?" she asked at once.

He said he was Dr. Ross. He said he was a psychiatrist.

"So then I *am* crazy," she said.

"No. I don't think so."

"I tried to kill myself."

"Right."

"So?"

"So that doesn't make you crazy. Very upset, yes. Disturbed, yes. But not crazy."

Carrie sat up and looked him over. "Then what are *you* here for?" She sounded rude. She knew she did, but she didn't really care.

"I'm here to see if together we can make you feel better."

Carrie lay back against the pillow and studied him warily. She wondered if what he said could be true. "I'm not just anemic, you know. That's not it. That's what my parents thought."

"No. You're right, it's not that."

"So what will you do to me?" she said cautiously. She had read about horrible things that psychiatrists did.

"We'll talk."

"That's all?"

He nodded.

"Am I going to stay in this hospital?"

"For a while."

"And be guarded by nurses?"

"Do you think you need to be?"

"No," Carrie said.

"Okay, then. No nurses." As if he had really listened to her and believed what she said.

Carrie kept looking at him. She studied him closely. She never could say—ever—why she decided to trust him, but at that moment she decided that she would. And as if she were offering him a present, she said very softly, "Would you like me to tell you about the island?"

And he said, "Yes, if you want to do that." And that was how it began.

It began that way, but it wasn't always like that. Some days she didn't want to talk. She wanted to drift and float and forget where she was. He wouldn't let her.

There were days when they sat with silence like a brick wall between them. Other days she couldn't stop talking.

Little by little a heaviness began to lift from between her shoulders. One afternoon he asked if she would like to go home for Christmas.

"To stay?"

"If it works well."

"Am I cured?" she asked doubtfully.

"Well, let's say that we still have lots of talking to do, but I think we can do it in my office."

Carrie looked down at her hands, folded in her lap. "I'll have to think about it," she said.

Another afternoon she said, "About going home—I'm afraid."

"Of?"

"Being there."

And two days later. "It's not being there so much, it's whether being there will make it all happen again."

"Do you think it will?"

"I don't know."

And another day. "Do you think I'll ever really be better?"

"Yes. You will get better a little at a time."

There was still a week left until Christmas. In the nurses' station someone had set up a little tree, and there were twin holly wreaths on the doors to the sun-room. Carrie sometimes sat there to watch television, and, of course, the television programs were full of Christmas, too. She thought back on all the Christmases she could remember, and one day she asked him, "If I did go home and it happened again, what would I do?"

"Any time that you're worried you can call me."

"And I'll see you again right after Christmas?"

"The next day."

"I'll have to think some more," she said.

After he left, she stood at the window of her room and looked down a shaft into the parking lot below. She stood there a long time. After a while she saw him come around the corner into the lot and get into a car. Even five floors above she could hear the ignition turn over. She watched until he had pulled out of sight.

It reminded her of standing at the big front window in the old apartment, watching her parents' car pull away from the curb. She'd watch as long as she could see it and then continue watching long after the last red blink of the taillights had vanished, in case, for some reason, they came back. She'd always worried that they might not come back.

But she would trust him. He would come back. "And I can call him any time," she said aloud. And then she went down to the nurses' station and told them that she thought she'd be going home for Christmas.

◦15◦

Her mother was coming for her after breakfast. It was the day before Christmas Eve. A nurse had packed her robe and toothbrush, her books and the few other things she'd had at the hospital. Then she offered to help Carrie dress. Carrie refused. It seemed silly to be treated like a patient now, when in an hour or so she would be home.

Dressed, she sat on the visitor's chair with her bag at her feet and waited for her mother. Her clothes felt strange after she had worn pajamas for a month. Her hands were cold. She clasped them tightly together around the paper with telephone numbers Dr. Ross had given her. She was afraid.

She didn't know what it would be like. In the hospital it seemed all right to be troubled. At home she wasn't sure. She closed her eyes and imagined that Dr. Ross was there. She imagined that his was the hand she clasped.

Her mother's heels made a clicking noise as she came down the corridor. She was in a hurry. Carrie had noticed that the hospital made her mother nervous and, now that they could leave, her mother wanted to do it immediately. "Packed?" she said, car keys jingling on her finger. Carrie nodded. They stopped for a minute to say good-bye to the nurses at the desk, and then they were in the elevator.

Carrie stood stiffly as they descended. I can call him any time, she repeated silently.

"We're parked in the lot across the street," her mother said. "Is your bag heavy?"

"There's almost nothing in it," Carrie answered. And then the revolving door spun her into a wall of cold air so abruptly that she caught her breath.

They crossed the salted sidewalk and the street, bent against the wind. "Moira has gone to Chicago with the choir," her mother said, slamming the car door. "They're singing at some hospital."

"Does she know I'm coming home today?"

"Yes, of course. Everyone knows."

"You mean you've been telling people?"

"The family is what I mean."

Her mother began backing the car out of the parking space. "It's slippery today," she said.

"What about everyone else? Are you still telling them I've just been sick?"

"Well, you have been. I don't know what else you'd call it."

"Not that."

"Carrie, please. We're going home. I don't see why we need to dwell on it. Let's call it an unfortunate incident. It's over now. It's almost Christmas."

"It isn't over, you know. I'm going to see Dr. Ross five days a week."

"Yes, but that's kind of like having checkups. That's how I see it."

Carrie didn't answer. She rested her cheek against the cold car window and watched the cross streets they passed, heading home.

Her mother stopped in front of the house, at a path that had been shoveled to the front door. Carrie followed up the path, hugging her bag. The house was silent. "Isn't anyone home?" Carrie said.

"They're here somewhere."

Carrie stood for a moment before taking off her coat, looking around the front hall. It seemed both familiar and strange. On the hall table was a large red azalea in florist's foil. Grouped under it were their little china Christmas angels.

"Why are the angels out here?" Carrie asked. "Why not on the mantel?"

"Oh, Carrie, they've gotten so shabby. They're so old."

Carrie's angel stood next to Moira's, firmly holding her harp to her chest. Carrie picked her up and cradled her in her hand.

"You see the chips in her wings?"

"That's from once when Duncan was trying to make her fly."

"I guess so. I forget. His is the worst, anyway."

"I wish they were on the mantel."

Her mother looked up from unzipping her boots. "We saved doing the tree until you got home."

Carrie replaced the angel and picked up her bag. The tree had nothing to do with the angel, she thought. She had said something, and her mother had answered something else.

This, too, seemed both strange and familiar.

"I think I'll go and unpack," Carrie said. "I want to see my room."

She climbed the stairs slowly, thinking how many weeks it had been since she'd climbed them and how long it was since she'd slept in her room. In the upstairs hall she stopped again to look around and then went through her own doorway.

The room seemed unnaturally tidy. It looked like a bedroom kept for guests. The chair where she piled her books was empty. The cushion was plumped, and there were vacuum sweeper tracks in the carpet. The bathroom door was closed. Carrie left it closed and put her toothbrush on the desk.

She found a hanger in the closet for her robe. Her skirts were lined up there in plastic dry cleaner's bags, her sweaters folded neatly on the shelf. The closet smelled of mothballs.

She unpacked the books and set them in a precise stack on her desk, careful as a visitor. She had pressed one of Mrs. Ramsay's carnations between the pages of a novel. She took it out and sniffed it. The scent was gone, changed to something vaguely unpleasant. She held the flower against her cheek for a moment before she threw it in the wastebasket. Then, carefully, she tucked Dr. Ross's numbers under a pad of paper in her desk.

"Carrie?" Duncan was standing hesitantly in the doorway.

"Hi, Duncan."

"Hi." He leaned awkwardly against the doorjamb. "Did you get the card I made you?"

"Sure I did. I liked it. Didn't Mother tell you?"

"I would've come to see you, only they said I couldn't."

"I know." Carrie sat down on the bed. "Why don't you come all the way in?"

Duncan took a step into the room and stood clumsily with his hands behind him.

"Sit down or something," Carrie said.

"I made you another card." From behind his back Duncan produced a large folded piece of red construction paper. "Red and green for Christmas, see?"

Carrie took the card. Duncan had drawn a circle of holly leaves on the front in green crayon. Inside the circle he had printed: "Welcome Home."

"It's really nice," said Carrie, and then, "Thank you."

"Well," said Duncan, "That's how I feel."

"Why don't you sit down for a minute?"

Duncan lowered himself to the carpet, still hesitant. "Do you feel funny around me?" Carrie said. "Because of what happened?"

Duncan drew a circle on the carpet with his fingertip, then another. "I wish you didn't get so sick," he said. "Did you get sick because of my hockey game?"

"No. Of course not. Why do you say that?"

"Sophie said maybe you got too cold walking there."

"It didn't have anything to do with that, Duncan." Carrie looked at his skinny little finger, tracing circles. "What happened was—" she began and then stopped. She didn't know how to tell him. "It wasn't that, Duncan, honestly. It was something else."

"I know," Duncan said softly, all hunched over. "Moira told me finally."

"Oh, Dunc!"

Carrie scrambled off the bed and dropped to the floor. She put her arms around him. Sitting on the carpet, she held him tight against her. He didn't cry. He didn't say anything at all. But they sat that way until Sophie called them to lunch.

"I made mushroom soup—homemade," Sophie said. "That's what you need to put some weight on you."

"I'm not skinny," said Carrie. She sat down at her place between her father and mother and across from Duncan.

"I don't know how Sophie has time to make soup with all the Christmas cooking," their mother said.

"For Carrie she has time," said their father.

Carrie floated her spoon across the surface of the soup, skimming little pools of melted butter.

"I'll bet you never had anything this good at the hospital," her father said. "At least I've never seen it."

"No," Carrie said. "The soup there is watery."

Duncan, who hated mushrooms, bit into his peanut butter sandwich. "Did you have peanut butter?"

"Duncan, your mouth is full," their mother said.

"I never had any," Carrie said. "Lunch is more like dinner there."

"Mystery meat, that's what they serve," said her father.

" 'Mystery' because you can't tell what kind of animal it came from."

Carrie's mother settled her spoon beside her plate. "We're all glad Carrie's home," she said. "But don't you think we've talked enough about the hospital? After all, it's nearly Christmas Eve and we haven't discussed our plans at all. When will we do the tree?"

Carrie watched the mushrooms floating in her soup plate. Someplace just behind her eyes she knew that the island was floating. Careful. Carefully she filled her spoon and lifted it to her mouth. Carefully she lowered it. "Tonight?" she said. "Could we do it after dinner?"

"Fine with me," said her father.

Each small event, each person, seemed to Carrie like a tiny bridge to cross. But it would get better, a little at a time, as Dr. Ross had said. And if not, she could call. She lowered her spoon into the soup again and remembered the folded paper with the telephone numbers lying safe in her desk drawer.

Sophie invited Carrie and Duncan to decorate cookies after the lunch dishes were done. Waiting, Carrie wandered into the living room and stood at the bay window looking out at the street. A space had been made between the chairs in the bay for the tree to stand. Her mother had arranged boughs of evergreen and glittering gold balls on the mantel. It looked pretty, but strange that way.

Carrie went into the hall and picked up her angel. She *was* shabby. Big patches of glaze were missing from her wings, and a brownish crack zigzagged up her middle. Carrie stroked her with an index finger. "Poor thing," she said. She carried the angel into the living room and set her on the mantel.

◦16◦

Moira didn't come home until nearly five o'clock. By then the cookies were finished and set out in rows in the pantry. The house was full of the buttery smell of them.

Carrie heard Moira come in the side door, stomp off snow, and say something to Sophie. Then she heard her start upstairs. She went out into the hall to meet her.

"Carrie, hi!" Moira's cheeks were flushed, and the hair along her forehead had flattened into damp ringlets. "Welcome home."

Moira looked beautiful. Carrie had forgotten how beautiful she was.

"Did you have to walk from school?"

"I got a ride partway. But it's cold!" Then, reaching the top of the stairs, "How are you?"

"I'm all right."

"You look great."

"Actually I look awful," Carrie said.

Moira ran her fingers through her damp hair. "Come talk to me while I change my clothes."

Carrie followed her down the hall. As if by mutual agreement they avoided the shortcut through Carrie's room and the bathroom. Moira flipped on her desk lamp. "Dark December," she said. "I hate it."

Carrie sat on the window seat and watched her shed her plaid skirt and pale blue shetland. Outside, snow was falling steadily again, past the streetlamp, past the lighted windows across the street. "Somebody moved into Mrs. Padmore's," Carrie said, suddenly registering the lights there.

"About two weeks ago. The kids have started at Sylvester."

"What an awful time to transfer."

"Yeah, but they're doing fine. The one in my class—Matt—is a real fox."

"Matt?"

"Matthew. He's about six feet two, and he has this really funny sense of humor." Moira pulled on a pair of jeans. "And then there's Daniel. He's in eighth grade. Probably he'll be in some of your classes. He isn't especially good looking, though—kind of funny looking." Moira glanced up. "Where's my brush? Did you use it?"

Carrie shook her head.

"Well, it has to be someplace around here," Moira said, and began searching, first in her bureau drawers, then in her purse, under her clothes piled at the foot of the bed, even on her night table.

"It's probably in the bathroom," said Carrie.

Moira looked up. She looked at Carrie and nodded. "Probably."

"It's all right," Carrie said. "It won't bother me."

Moira opened the bathroom door and switched on the light without replying. For the first time, Carrie saw the white tiles again. Deliberately she stood up and walked to the door of the bathroom. Deliberately she looked down at the floor and waited, but nothing happened. She felt nothing at all. Moira slammed the medicine cabinet shut. "I found it."

Carrie went back to the bedroom. "How has it been at school?" she asked.

"Oh, you know, exams."

"But about me, how has it been?"

Moira came back into the bedroom, shutting the door. "Nobody knows about you."

"They really believe I've had some kind of bronchitis? For a whole month?"

"I think so. We haven't said anything else, and people don't ask a lot of questions."

"You told Duncan."

"I *had* to tell Duncan. He felt guilty."

"And you must have said something to Mrs. Ramsay. She sent me flowers."

"I said you were in the hospital with bronchitis."

"That's what Mother wants to say, isn't it? About bronchitis."

Moira nodded.

"In fact that's what she wants to believe, isn't it? She doesn't want to remember I took pills."

"Carrie, don't."

"Well, I *did*, Moira. That's what I did."

"Don't think I don't know it!" Moira whirled around. All at once her face was fierce with anger. "I'm the one who found you!"

"Oh." Carrie dropped back onto the window seat. "I'm sorry."

"It's a good thing somebody found you."

"I didn't know who it was. Nobody said."

"They don't like to talk about it." Moira sat down on the edge of the bed and looked at the floor, swinging her hairbrush between her knees. "Neither do I."

"You're mad at me."

"Well, Carrie, it's been hard on all of us. Think about it."

"I know."

Carrie got up and went to sit beside her sister. She couldn't hug her the way she had Duncan and so she reached out and touched her hair.

"Don't."

"We're going to trim the tree after dinner," Carrie said. "Sophie's making her usual horrible eggnog."

"I have to go to a party tonight," Moira said flatly.

"Oh. I thought everybody'd be home."

Moira stood up and began brushing her hair hard, leaning forward so that it fell over her face in a bright, heavy mass. Carrie remembered a Christmas in Chicago when she'd brushed Moira's hair, trying to brush out the kinks her braids made so that she could be an angel in the Christmas play. "I wish we still lived in Chicago," she said.

Moira flung back her hair. It stood out wildly, electrified. "Why?"

"Because it was nice there. Remember how little our Christmas trees were? Remember they were so little you and I could put the star on top?"

Moira smiled. "I remember when you tipped the whole tree over doing it."

Carrie chuckled. "Yeah." She lay back across the bed and looked at the snow falling, upside down. After a while Moira said, "I guess I wouldn't have to go tonight, or I could go late."

"It's your year to hang the lamb," Carrie said, "and you can hang the snowman, too, if you want."

"Oh, let's let Duncan do those."

"Really?"

"Sure. He's still little."

Then Moira put a record on her stereo and went down the hall to telephone. Carrie lay spread-eagled. The rhythmic pulse of a bass guitar vibrated against her ear through the mattress. She hated that music.

She closed her eyes, and for a part of a second then, and without warning, she saw it. A piece of the island. Hot flat rocks. Then the room again. She sat up at once. When Moira returned, she stood up to go.

In the doorway she paused. "Moira?"

Moira turned down the volume in order to hear.

"I'm not going to lie if someone asks me," she said.

"I'm going to tell them the truth. I have to."

"*Why* do you have to? Can't you just let it drop?"

"I won't bring it up, but if someone asks I won't lie. I have to be myself," she said finally, "and doing what I did—that's part of me."

After dinner their father carried the tree in and set it in the space that had been cleared in the living room. Carrie and Moira, as they had done for years, sat one on either side of the ornament box, unwrapping stars and strings of tinsel from wads of old protective tissue paper. For the first time Duncan was in charge of the lights. He was taking it seriously, squatting among the tangle of cords, testing bulbs.

"Look," Carrie said, "the drum you made, Duncan." She lifted the little cardboard drum out of its wrappings to show him.

"We made those in third grade."

"I'd forgotten that drum," their mother said. "Someplace in there are the Santas you girls made in Mrs. Stanton's class. I think there are two of them. She must have had her children do Santas every year."

"She did," said Moira. "Mrs. Stanton wasn't overloaded with imagination."

"She was nice, though," Carrie said. "I remember when Tanya wet her pants in the art room. Mrs. Stanton didn't bawl her out or anything."

"She wet her pants?" Duncan stopped testing lights and looked at Carrie. "In third grade?"

"She couldn't help it."

"Boy, if anyone did that when I was in third grade, people would still be kidding them."

"No, they wouldn't."

"They would, too! Anyone who did that would have to be a real weirdo, and you know how kids are about weirdies." Then Duncan stopped talking suddenly and began tightening a bulb.

"I'm going to get the eggnog," their mother said. "Do we want cookies now, or is it too soon after dinner?"

Even her father turned from straightening the tree and smiled at Carrie.

Carrie flattened a piece of tissue paper on her knee and studied the pattern the wrinkles made crisscrossing. She might save the paper and draw it, she thought—draw all the wrinkles and tears and name the drawing, simply, "Tissue Paper." She would have to get used to the things they said. They would say lots of things and mean no harm.

"Aren't you going to help me?" Moira said.

"Yes, I was thinking." Carrie wadded up the paper and stuffed it in her back pocket.

"What are you saving that for?"

"To draw."

"On?"

"No. I'm going to draw *it*."

The paper and the angel and herself—all of them a little ragged. But, Carrie thought, it's okay. It had to be okay. She looked up at her angel on the mantel and was pleased to see her mother had left it there among all the shining balls.

·17·

Christmas. The house smelled of turkey. In the morning the sun shone and they sat beside the tree in their robes, opening the mounds of packages that had appeared overnight. Later in the afternoon it grew cloudy. Their mother began switching on lamps.

Duncan lay sprawled on the floor watching their father feed little handfuls of wrapping paper to the fire. "Anyone want to play backgammon?" he asked.

"I don't," said Moira.

"I didn't mean you, creep. You never want to do anything." He began gouging at the living room carpet with the toe of his shoe.

"Duncan, don't," their mother said automatically.

"It's true. All Moira wants to do is listen to records and hang around the boys."

"I do *not* hang around anyone."

"Please," said their mother.

"Christmas afternoon is the most boring time in the whole year," said Duncan.

"What a silly thing for you to say," their mother replied. "Christmas is lovely all day long."

But Duncan was right, Carrie thought. There was always the slow, stale letdown as Christmas afternoon coasted toward evening. Often her parents invited friends for drinks late Christmas Day. This year they hadn't. She glanced from one of them to the other, wondering if she was the reason. She wanted to say, "It'd be all right. Go ahead.

Nothing will happen," but there wasn't any way to do that.

It would be better if they could talk about it, she thought—so much better. It was as if there were a great ugly box in the middle of the room which everybody stepped around but would not admit was there.

"I think I'll put my presents away," she said.

They were safe presents mostly, Carrie thought, the kinds of things you might buy for someone you didn't know well. She laid them on the bed: A shetland sweater—navy blue; a bottle of cologne; a matching knitted cap and scarf from Aunt Louise; four pairs of knee socks; a macrame belt; and a book called *Masterpieces from the Louvre*. Thoughtfully she studied them.

From Moira's room came the thump and throb of a bass guitar. The music seemed to be crawling in under the bathroom door. Carrie tried not to hear it, but there was no possibility of that. She put her hands to her ears. The music crept through the cracks in her fingers. She hummed but, under and through the humming, she could hear the guitar.

It made her think of dark places and dampness. There was something about the way it pushed and insisted that reminded her of sweaty Katherine Fowles. She hated hearing it. She jumped up and opened the door on her side of the bathroom. "Turn that down!"

The stereo went quiet. Moira opened her door. "Well, good Lord, Carrie, you don't have to get mad."

"I hate that rotten music."

"Okay. Okay. I'll play something else."

Too agreeable. It wasn't like Moira to be that way. She's

afraid I'll flip out again, Carrie thought, and felt ashamed.

She sat down at her desk. In a minute she heard the voice of Neil Diamond. That was better. She relaxed.

After a while she pulled out a sketch pad and her charcoal pencils.

Idly she began to sketch the wing of shadow her books cast onto the blotter. It was the first time she'd drawn anything since before it all happened. She wondered whether she could still draw at all. And beneath that question, another more frightening question bobbed: Was she going to be all right? How could she know that it wouldn't happen again?

She thought of Moira's face. Moira wasn't sure. And I'm not sure, Carrie thought. All she could do was believe it would be better if she was patient and waited day by day.

She bent over the paper, drawing shadows—the shadow of the lampshade, the splayed shadows of pencils in a cup. For three days now it had been all right. Nearly all right. Each day would be better. And someday, she told herself fiercely, I will be well.

She sketched until dark, realizing it was dark only when she turned to look out the window and saw her own reflection in the black pane. She closed the sketchbook and got up to put her presents away. Among them, the big glossy art book caught her eye. The book touched her. She could imagine her mother standing perplexed in Marshall Field's book department, telling the salesman that her daughter liked art. She could have chosen a more unusual book, but Carrie liked it that she'd tried. She flipped open the book.

She was surprised to see that on the flyleaf her mother had written, "For my dear Carrie."

After a while Carrie went downstairs. Duncan and her father were watching a football game in the library. Her mother was in the kitchen.

"Do you want some help?" Carrie said.

Her mother turned. "That would be nice. I was going to make sandwiches and you could butter bread."

Carrie took a package of butter from the refrigerator, picked up a knife.

"No, use the soft butter. You'll tear holes in the bread spreading that."

Her mother had tied one of Sophie's aprons over her dress. It made her look different, Carrie thought. She looked the way she had years and years ago in Chicago.

Carrie flattened the knife blade and smoothed butter across a slice of bread. Her mother cut turkey. She was good at it—quick and deft—although she worked in the kitchen only on Sophie's days off now.

"This reminds me of watching you cook when we were little," Carrie said. "Remember how Moira and I used to sit on the kitchen stools?"

Her mother smiled. "I was always afraid one of you would fall off."

"I liked Chicago," Carrie said.

"Don't you like Northpoint better, though?"

Carrie didn't answer. After a while she said, "Remember in first grade, my school program? I wanted you to wear your evening dress and you wouldn't?"

"The program was at ten in the morning!"

"I understand that now, but then I just wanted you to wear your most beautiful dress. I thought you looked like a fairy princess in that dress."

"Oh, Carrie." Her mother put down the knife and wiped her hands on Sophie's apron. "That's nice." Then, awkwardly, she touched Carrie's arm.

"I told Dr. Ross about that once."

"Let's not talk about bad things."

"I guess I don't think about it as all bad," Carrie said, surprising herself. But it was true. There was some part of the experience—the pills, the hospital, the fear, even—that she realized she didn't think of as bad.

"Well, I do," her mother said in a small, tight voice. She began slicing turkey again.

Carrie returned to buttering bread. She felt as if she had seen a flower open and close. "I'm sorry I've worried you so much," she said quietly.

"I wish we could begin to forget it," her mother said. "That's all I really wish."

◇ 18 ◇

The day after Christmas Carrie's appointments began and, two days after New Year's, school. She dreaded going back.

"Nobody *knows*," Moira said as they turned the corner

to Sylvester. "Just remember that and you won't worry."

Carrie hitched up her book bag. It felt strange on her shoulder. It was not so much whether people knew that worried her. It was the dread that somehow it might happen again. But she couldn't say that. She glanced at Moira. She wished that she could stay near her all day.

"Listen," Moira said as they pushed through the doors. "I know it'll be all right. Really."

Carrie watched her disappear, flashing bright through the crowds of students like a fish darting through seaweed. Then Carrie went to her own locker, which was exactly as it had been, hung up her coat, and started to first-hour class.

Katherine Fowles swiveled around in her chair and said, "Welcome back. You sure must have been sick."

Carrie didn't answer.

"You missed a lot. How are you ever going to make up all the work?"

"I don't know. I will."

"I sure wouldn't want to be you," Katherine said and then, surprisingly, she smiled a little. "Well, anyway, welcome back."

The morning went by exactly as it always had. Carrie realized that nobody was much interested in where she'd been. Susan Rogers asked how she was feeling. A few people said, "Welcome." The teachers gave her make-up work to do on weekends. At lunch she sat at the table eating her sandwich, and listened to the chatter as she always had.

"It wasn't bad," she told Dr. Ross. "It wasn't good either. It was—" She shrugged. "It was just Sylvester."

And that was the way the week continued, as if nothing at all had changed.

It snowed a great deal that week, nearly every day. Four-foot mountains of it lined the streets where the plows had piled it. The roads were scarcely cleaned before they drifted over again. No one could remember snow like that before.

On the Saturday after school began, Carrie called Mrs. Ramsay about her lessons. She felt awkward calling. She needed to apologize for that day in the art room. She needed to explain. But Mrs. Ramsay made it easy for her. "I can't wait to see you! Come for lunch. I was in Milwaukee over Christmas vacation, or I'd have called you by now myself."

Carrie made her bed. She helped Duncan clean up his room, and then, at eleven, bundled in boots and scarf and her down jacket, she was ready to go.

"Will you call when you start home?" Her mother stood in the front hall, fidgeting with a gold bracelet.

"If you want me to." Her mother was still nervous about her going out alone.

"There's such a lot of snow."

"I'll be okay."

She set out walking. She followed a tire track for several blocks, then the track turned right and Carrie waded ahead, breaking her own path in an unplowed street until another set of tracks appeared. She had started out early so that she could stop in the Village at Byrd's Bookstore.

All morning the idea of taking a present to Mrs. Ramsay

had been on her mind—a late Christmas present or something like that. She knew it should be a book of drawings or paintings. It was only a matter of finding the right one.

There were long tables in Byrd's filled with books marked down after Christmas. One whole table contained art books. They were all beautiful, Carrie thought. A lot of them cost more than she had to spend, which narrowed the choice somewhat, but still there were many, and suddenly she felt shy about choosing.

She turned the pages of a volume of Canaletto reproductions slowly, lost for a moment in his clear, sunlit world of color. To her the pictures were marvelous, but would Mrs. Ramsay like them, or would she prefer something else? Carrie hesitated, checking the price on the jacket flap, and her eye fell on another book nearby. It was a volume of Beardsley drawings.

Reluctantly Carrie picked up the book and looked at the price. She could afford it. She was quite sure it was something Mrs. Ramsay would like. She flipped it open and recognized the style again at once—the twisting curve and recurve of line. As at the Art Institute, at first the line was all that she saw, and she followed it for several pages before she began really to look at the pictures. They were grotesque. Something was going on in these pictures, something was hidden here that she couldn't understand. She laid the book back on the table and turned to the Canaletto again, but it was too late.

A roaring. The corner of the island heaved up before her.

Where a second before there had been books of paintings, glossy and luxurious, now the flat, hot rocks of the island appeared. The fish circled in the water.

Carrie stood very still. She held tight to the edge of the table and breathed slowly. Slowly. She could stand there for a long time. There was no need to move. And so she stood and held on, and gradually the books began to reappear, one by one, swimming up like fish to the surface of the table.

Carrie stood quite still until she was sure it was over. Inside her jacket her shirt felt damp, and her face, she realized, was wet with perspiration. Nobody had noticed. Possibly it had lasted only a second. People milled behind her, calling out to children, laughing, asking prices.

Carrie picked up the Canaletto and headed for the cash register, and when the girl behind the counter asked whether she'd like to have the book gift-wrapped, Carrie was able to say, "Yes, please," like any other shopper.

But she wasn't like any other shopper. She stood outside the bookstore in the glitter of sun, holding her package and trembling. Dr. Ross had said it might happen again, and that if it did, she should call him. It might happen many times more, he said, but she knew now that it would go away if she waited. "Wait," he'd said. "Stay quiet and wait, and when it's over, then call me."

There was a telephone booth on the next corner. Carrie deposited her package on the floor and forced the glass door closed against the snowy transom. She knew the number and dialed it. Dr. Ross answered at once. No secretary. No answering service like her father's. Carrie was startled.

"It happened again," she said simply. "In the book-store."

"And what did you do?"

"I waited like you said. It went away."

"Do you have any idea what started it? What you were feeling?"

She told him about the Beardsley book, but she couldn't tell him what she'd been feeling. She didn't know what it was she was feeling.

Outside, people brushed past the booth. Cars crept down the snowy street, going slowly. Carrie spoke hesitantly, trying to explain what she didn't understand.

"But what you did worked, Carrie."

"Yes."

"So, if it happens again, you can handle it again."

"Yes."

"Okay, then," he said and it really did seem to be okay then. For that moment at least, for the next little bit of time.

Carrie pushed out of the booth. The telephone jingled inwardly, swallowing her money, and she began to go south on Main, walking in the direction of Mrs. Ramsay's.

° 19 °

"Carrie! Carrie! Come in! Get warm!" Mrs. Ramsay was standing at the front door. Over her painting jeans she was wearing a baggy man's cardigan many sizes too large. She stood hugging herself against the cold and grinning at Carrie wading her way up the narrow shoveled path to the door.

"The children did the shoveling," Mrs. Ramsay said. "It leaves something to be desired."

There was a fire in the living room grate burning fitfully. Sunlight cut a wide track across the rug.

Carrie came in, shed her coat and boots, and then, shyly, held out her package. "For you," she said.

"To open now?"

"It's a late Christmas present. You can open it now if you want."

Mrs. Ramsay carried the package into the living room and sat down in the faded old wing chair. She made an elaborate production of undoing the ribbon, opening the wrapping paper. "Oh, Canaletto," she said softly, lifting the book from the wrapping. "Oh, how lovely."

"I hoped you'd like it."

"How could I *help* liking it?" Mrs. Ramsay looked up and smiled, but there were tears in her eyes. She pulled a Kleenex from her pocket and dabbed at them. "I'm so touched and glad to see you I'm crying," she said.

Carrie stood awkwardly, uncomfortable at seeing a grown person cry, but Mrs. Ramsay didn't seem embarrassed. She blew her nose, dabbed at her eyes again, and opened the book. "I don't want to drip on this beautiful thing," she said.

Carrie went over and curled up in a corner of the sofa.

Dust motes drifted in the sunlight between them. As it always did, the room seemed to fold comfort around her. She looked about her at the familiar shelves of books, the crooked slipcovers, the dried cattails in a jar on the mantel. Part of a jigsaw puzzle lay finished on the coffee table and, beside it, an ashtray containing a broken string of beads. The log sparked and crumbled noisily. Carrie stretched and felt herself beginning to grow easy. She felt the moment in the bookstore fading, growing dim as if it had happened days before.

The Ramsays' cat leaped onto the sofa and curled himself next to Carrie. She stroked his fur with her fingertips, feeling his purr like a motor under the skin. Mrs. Ramsay got up to poke the fire.

"Shall we have lunch here, do you think? Or shall we be grand and eat in the dining room?"

"In here."

"That's what I think, too."

They carried plates and cups in from the kitchen and had tuna-fish sandwiches and tea before the fire. Mrs. Ramsay talked about the children, about Christmas. She asked whether Carrie was drawing. "There's another contest in the spring," she said. "You might like to enter it."

Carrie broke off a bit of sandwich and fed the cat. "We should be hearing about the other competition soon, shouldn't we?"

Mrs. Ramsay didn't answer, and Carrie looked up. "Or have you already heard?" she said.

"Yes. About a month ago."

"I didn't do so well, right?"

"You didn't win anything. I'm sorry, Carrie. I wish you had."

Carrie let the cat lick her fingertips with his rough tongue. She smiled at Mrs. Ramsay. "It's okay," she said. "I never expected to win. I don't think I'm too disappointed." And this was true, she thought. She could scarcely remember the drawings she'd done in the fall. It was as if they belonged to another person.

"I'd like to see you enter the spring competition. If you *feel* like entering, of course." And then, "How *do* you feel, Carrie?"

Carrie looked down at the cat. She gave him a last tiny bit of crust. She shrugged. "Right now I feel fine. But other times not so good."

"Tell me about it. If you want to tell me, I mean."

"I don't mind telling you, but I don't know if I can. Here, you see, here in this house with you it's all right, but other places it isn't. Other places I feel like a stranger."

Mrs. Ramsay nodded as if she understood what Carrie meant.

"Like this puzzle." Carrie pointed to the half-finished jigsaw puzzle on the coffee table. "All the pieces fit together because they belong to the same puzzle. But a piece from another puzzle would never fit. That's me. I feel like that kind of puzzle piece."

Mrs. Ramsay leaned back in the wing chair and gazed

thoughtfully at the fireplace, where a single bluish flame struggled at the end of the log. "Everybody belongs to the same puzzle, Carrie."

Carrie frowned, nesting her empty teacup between her palms. "When I was little, it was different," she said.

"How do you mean?"

Carrie looked at the cat and at the flicker of the firelight and at the chipped spout of the china teapot on the coffee table. "When we were little," she said, "Moira and I would spend whole afternoons together lying in the sun beside our fish pond. We'd lean over the edge and call the fish. We had this secret language for calling them. Well, I wish nothing had ever changed, that's all. I wish we could just lie there forever, calling fish."

"You didn't feel like a loose jigsaw piece then."

"No, I didn't. It was like being here."

Mrs. Ramsay didn't say anything. She made some vague motions toward picking up empty plates. This didn't feel like an interruption.

"But everything changed," Carrie said. "And then last fall these queer, awful things began to happen in my head."

Mrs. Ramsay nodded. "I know."

"I'm sorry about that day in the art room. It happened then. I couldn't help it."

"One day it'll feel all right again."

"I don't know."

"I promise."

After a while they gathered up the plates and cups and carried them to the kitchen. The sun had retracted to a pale patch on the windowsill. Carrie glanced at the clock. "I'd probably better go," she said.

Halfway into her jacket she stopped and turned. "*How* did you know about what happened?" she asked. "I never told you."

"Your mother told me."

"My *mother?*"

"I went over to see her when you were in the hospital. I think she needed to talk to someone."

Carrie couldn't think of anything to say. She stopped to pull on her boots. "She won't even talk to *me* about it," she said finally.

"Maybe she will someday," Mrs. Ramsay said. "She loves you very much."

Partway up the block Carrie remembered she'd promised to call when she started home. Well, it was too late to go back. She turned up the collar of her jacket and trudged on.

Her mother had told Mrs. Ramsay? Why had she done that? "She loves you very much." Carrie thought about Mrs. Ramsay's words. She dug her fists into the pockets of her jacket. She turned left.

At the corner by the Standard station she stopped and waited for a car to pass. The drugstore across the street was already lighted, although the clock inside said just past three-thirty. Under the clock Carrie saw a pay phone. She pushed through the glass doors into the warmth of the store. In the phone booth she rooted for coins again and dialed home. Sophie answered.

"Sophie, tell Mother I'm on my way, will you, please?

Tell her I'll be home in about ten minutes." And then Carrie pushed back out into the gray afternoon.

·20·

The last block from home it began snowing, occasional fat flakes that drifted slowly toward the ground like cottonwood seeds in summer. Carrie caught one on her tongue.

Up ahead, a car was stalled in the middle of the street. Two figures in parkas were pushing from behind, shouting instructions to an invisible driver. Coming closer, Carrie saw Moira standing on the curb, watching. Carrie came up beside her.

"How could they get stuck there?" she said. "It's flat."

"No snow tires."

Carrie looked at the two boys straining behind the car. "Why are you standing here?"

"I just came out to watch."

"To watch a stuck car? What for?"

Moira gave her a look that was part irritated, part embarrassed. "That's the Spanglers," she said.

"Who?"

"The people from across the street. Remember, I told you?"

"Oh. The guy in your class."

Moira dug her chin into her scarf. "That's right."

"So are you going to help or what? I don't understand what you're doing out here."

Moira exhaled loudly, making a little frosty puff in the air. "Just never mind, okay?"

"Keep rocking it!" one of the boys yelled. The car rolled back and then lurched forward suddenly, spraying snow. "Keep going!" the boy shouted and the car slid ahead uncertainly but kept going. Both boys turned toward them, laughing.

"That's our mom," one of them said. "She's never driven much in snow before." He had a slight Southern accent.

"I suppose there isn't much snow in Virginia," Moira said.

"Not like this. Man!"

"This is my sister," Moira said. "Carrie, this is Matt Spangler and"—she hesitated—"Daniel—is that right?"

Daniel grinned at Carrie. "You got transferred into my math class," he said.

"I know. I recognize you."

"Everyone says you're good."

"Everyone in accelerated math is good."

Daniel kept smiling. It was a nice smile. "Supposed to be," he said, "but I sometimes wonder about myself."

"Oh, look! Jeez!" Matt exclaimed. "She's going to try to get up the driveway! Run!" And the two of them took off, running, calling, "Nice to meet you," over their shoulders in the general direction of Carrie.

"Good luck!" Moira called after them, but they were already out of earshot.

Carried followed Moira along the slit of sidewalk to the side door. "They're cute, don't you think?" Moira said.

"I guess so."

"So you already knew Daniel?"

"I've seen him in class."

They stomped off snow in the entry, and Carrie went upstairs to her room. She thought she would try to finish her history assignment before dinner. She had all the make-up assignments to do as well as new work. If she thought about it all at once, she felt overwhelmed. If I work at it, little by little, it'll get done, she thought, and sat down and opened the history text.

But instead of the words on the page, she suddenly saw herself clutching the table in Byrd's, perspiring, hanging on. How long had it been—a minute, two minutes? And why had it happened? Dr. Ross would ask her why again.

Carrie leaned forward on her elbows and stared at the ugly pink wallpaper above the desk. It had been the Beardsley book. Beardsley, the show at the Art Institute, the feelings she'd had there, what Mrs. Ramsay had said—that was what had made it happen today. The Beardsley book had reminded her of all that.

After a while she looked down at the history book again. She listened to Sophie clattering dishes. She sniffed the warm odor of pot roast that floated up from the kitchen. That was what she'd tell him when he asked her. Then she began reading about the Battle of Marathon.

112

Carrie worked hard all of January. She kept up with the class and managed the back work as well, so that by the time semester exams started at the end of January, she was ready to take them. It gave her great satisfaction to be caught up. It would give her more time to work on drawings, for one thing. Her drawing had suffered.

During the few days of semester break she began seriously to draw again. She felt rusty at first, as if she were starting almost from scratch. For practice, she set up a still life of pencils and books on her desk and sketched them for a time, then began to abstract the objects into simple geometric shapes again. She worked several weeks this way— through the first three weeks of February—thinking of the spring competition, but there was something in the drawings that didn't satisfy her. She felt puzzled.

"There's something I'm not getting right in these sketches," she said to Mrs. Ramsay.

It was Saturday morning. Outside the window icicles dripped. It was the January thaw, as Sophie said, a month late.

Mrs. Ramsay stopped her own sketching and stood up to look at Carrie's. "What's bothering you?"

"I can't tell."

Upstairs, Saskia began coughing. "I've got to give her her medicine and check the vaporizer," Mrs. Ramsay said. "Do you want some light? It seems awfully dim in here."

The light helped. Carrie looked at the sketch she'd been

doing, turned it this way and that critically, and knew she truly wasn't pleased. It was dead. Most of the work she'd been doing in the past month struck her that way. It was the deadness that made the drawings bad, and it worried her.

Mrs. Ramsay hadn't said so, but Carrie was certain that she saw it, too. The drawings were only patterns. Complicated patterns, but without interest. Carrie had not let herself think about it much, but at the back of her mind was the fear that this lifelessness was connected to all the rest that had happened. She was afraid that she had lost her talent and had somehow killed the part of herself that could draw.

She flipped over a new page on the sketch pad. Nothing she'd done since Christmas was half good enough to enter in the spring.

Mrs. Ramsay's drawing lay on the table next to her. She glanced at it. It was a seated figure—a man—and it was good. Carrie wondered whether it might be Mr. Ramsay. She'd never seen him, since he worked on Saturdays, but she supposed it was. She knew the picture was good without being able to say why. Something generous about it. Something warm. It was not dead, certainly—just the opposite.

She began to sketch again without plan. Mrs. Ramsay came back into the room and sat down. She looked at her own drawing critically. She rubbed at a charcoal line. "I looked at your drawing," Carrie said. "I like it."

"Well, his knee is bothering me."

"That's from a model?"

"No. Memory. Imagination."

"Is it Mr. Ramsay?" Carrie asked.

"Oh, I don't know. Just a man." Mrs. Ramsay frowned at the paper. "Listen, Saskia wants to know, will you draw her a picture?"

"What does she want?"

"Just anything. Give her something you've done that you don't want."

Carrie flipped through the sketch pad slowly. "I don't think there's anything here she'd like."

"She loves you. She'd like anything you've made."

"But they really aren't very good, are they?" Carrie said.

"They're not bad."

"But not good."

"They're marking-time pictures," Mrs. Ramsay said.

"I don't understand."

"They're transitional. They're what you're drawing until you find what you're looking for."

Carrie smoothed her hand across the sheet of paper, smearing the tentative line she'd drawn.

"Last fall I thought I'd found what I was looking for. I liked making a thing all shape and line. I didn't want to draw things the way they really looked. I wanted to draw what I saw inside my own head."

"So maybe now you want to do something different."

"But I don't know what it is."

Mrs. Ramsay got them some tea, and they went back to

their drawings. "You know, Carrie, I don't want you to feel compelled to enter anything this spring if you don't feel ready. There will be many more competitions."

"I'd like to try, though," Carrie said. "I don't know that I can do it. I don't know *what* I can do any more. But I'd like to try. The problem is, I can't count on myself the way I used to."

She realized that she had grown accustomed to knowing this. She allowed for uncertainty now in the same way she'd had to allow for her cast the year she broke her leg.

The room was quiet except for the dripping of icicles and the scratching of their charcoal. The silence was as companionable as conversation. Mrs. Ramsay began to whistle softly. Carrie sketched carelessly. The drawing taking shape on the paper seemed to be finding its direction without her.

"Carrie, did you make me a picture yet?" Saskia was standing in the dining room doorway in pajamas, holding a dirty shred of blanket against her cheek. Speaking made her start to cough again. She doubled over, getting red in the face.

"Honey, you're supposed to be up there with the vaporizer," Mrs. Ramsay said.

"I've been waiting a long time. I watched four cartoons, so that's an hour."

"Come and choose something," Carrie said. "I don't know what to give you."

Saskia padded across the rug on bare feet and clambered onto the table. "Let me look at them all." Carrie handed her the sketch pad.

One by one Saskia turned the pages, taking her time and looking at each drawing seriously. She held the book on her knees and leaned so close to the page that sometimes the tips of her hair grazed the paper. Occasionally she paused to cough.

She finally came to the last drawing on the pad. She looked for a time, then patted it. "This one."

"That's not even finished," Carrie said. "I just started it."

"I like it best, though."

"Why not any of the others?"

Saskia shrugged.

"No. I really want to know," Carrie said, "I think there's something wrong with them, too, but I can't tell what it is."

"No people," said Saskia.

Carrie was confused. "There aren't people in this new one, either."

"I know," Saskia said, "but there could be."

Carrie took the sketch pad and looked at the picture. To her astonishment, she saw that she had drawn the island.

◦22◦

From the beginning Carrie had taken the 3:30 train into Chicago for her appointments. When school began in January, it was a rush to make it. She had just fifteen minutes between the last bell and the train, and if she was even slightly delayed she had to run all the way to the station.

She grew used to the rush after a while and stopped minding it. At first she minded everything—the train, the taxis, the elevator ride, the talking itself. Often the long stumbling talks with Dr. Ross seemed to be going nowhere. She hated this. "I can't remember," she would reply to a question. Or, "I don't understand." She felt then as if a bare stretch of desert extended before her as far as she could see and that she would never be able to cross it.

"What's the use of all this?" she'd say. "I come and I talk, but what changes? What's better?" Then he would remind her of how it had been before, and she would have to admit it *was* better.

What was it like now? She had time to think about that, riding back and forth to Chicago. Gray, she decided. If the worst times had been garishly colored, then these days were, by comparison, gray.

At school nothing changed. She went to classes, did her work. Once Susan Rogers inquired where it was Carrie went after school, and Carrie, in panic, lied. "The dentist," she said. "My teeth are all shot." She'd said this in spite of her resolve to tell the truth. She dreaded being asked again.

At home, too, little changed. Moira had begun to go out with Matt Spangler. Duncan had a strep throat and recovered. Otherwise, things went on the same.

She and Dr. Ross talked about all this, not just once but endlessly. Moira, Duncan, her parents. Tanya, Mrs. Ramsay. They discussed Moira's music. Why did Carrie hate it? They talked about Beardsley. What did she see there? Why was she frightened? What did it mean?

Questions. There were days when the questions overwhelmed her. And, then, in early March, there was a new one. Why had she begun to draw the island?

Because that was what she'd been doing. Almost in spite of herself since that Saturday morning at Mrs. Ramsay's she had drawn it repeatedly. She'd tried not to. She had finally forced herself to go back again to still lifes, but even in the course of sketching them, the apples became rocks and moss and water.

It worried her. Just as she had had no control over the slipping in her head, now, it seemed, she could not resist drawing the island. Did it mean she would never be better? She asked Dr. Ross about this, but his answer was a question: "Is there any harm in drawing your island? That's different from being there, isn't it?" Yes. It was different. And so she drew it and drew it, and then one day she bought paints.

She hadn't intended to do that. She saw the paint box in a bookstore window, nestling among pads of paper and boxes of pastels, and she couldn't resist. It was the sort of box you'd buy for a child—colors in flat, dry cakes. Carrie couldn't stop looking. The colors were delicious, even the names of the colors—aquamarine, cerulean. Without pausing to think, she went into the store and bought them.

Between the small flat cakes of paints there was a brush.

At home Carrie licked the tip, moistened the cake of aquamarine and made a stroke of color on the back of her notebook.

Aquamarine. The color of water. "I bought them so I could paint the island," Carrie said matter-of-factly, as if she had known it all along. And then she flopped, stomach-down, on her bed and wondered for the millionth time why it was the island she wanted to paint.

"So now I'm painting it," she said to him.

"Oh?"

"But why?"

"Well, Carrie, what *is* the island? What does it mean to you?"

Over and over the same question, while she stared at the rabbit-shaped water stain above his head.

"I don't *know!* What *is* the island?" she said, throwing back the question in despair. "Why do you always ask? Why don't you ever answer?"

He never reacted to her anger. He just accepted it and waited, and after a while she calmed down.

"I can't tell you what the island is. You will have to tell us both," he said.

But she couldn't. She could only describe it. She leaned back in the chair and began again.

By late March she had a folder full of watercolors. One Friday she took them, together with half a dozen of her abstract drawings, to her appointment. In the taxi and again in the elevator she told herself she could change her mind, stuff them in her book bag and not mention she'd brought them. But, once in the office, she laid them on his desk.

"I brought these," she said, "to show you what I mean." Her voice, she thought, sounded stiff and unnatural, but she went on, "I can't explain the island as well as I can paint it. I thought that maybe if you looked at the pictures you could tell me why I keep on doing it."

He opened the folder and spread the pictures out on his desk. Carrie stood awkwardly across from him and concentrated on a tiny nick in the surface of the wood. She couldn't look at him looking. She would know instantly if he didn't like the pictures, and she didn't want to know that.

"They are very beautiful, aren't they?" he said after several minutes.

Carrie looked up hesitantly. She searched his eyes for something dishonest or uncomprehending, but there was nothing like that. He meant that the pictures were beautiful. She sat down slowly in the brown leather chair across from him. "I think they are," she said.

"And very complicated." His eyes behind his glasses were serious.

"Yes."

She paused. Even the sounds in the room were so familiar now that she scarcely noticed them. The clock clicked over. Dr. Ross struck a match. Her own voice rising and falling seemed to belong to the place.

He leaned forward, scattering ashes. "What can you tell me about painting them?" he said.

There it was again—a question! "What do you mean by that?" she said softly. And then, suddenly, she couldn't bear another question. She slammed forward. "You *know* I can't tell you anything else! That's why I brought the pictures to show you! So you'd help me! My father is paying you money to help me!"

She'd screamed at him. She'd sounded rude. Spoiled. She was ashamed.

The sound of her voice echoed and settled and died away. The clock clicked over. "I'm sorry," she said. He shrugged. It didn't matter. In this office it was all right to be rude. It was still hard for her to be used to that.

Raindrops began to spot the windowpane. "What about your sketches?" he said.

"Well, you can see what those are—patterns. I used to like them, but now I don't much. My family never did. They're relieved I've stopped doing them. I think they feel those pictures were a symptom or something. You know, first I started doing abstract drawings, and then I had all the trouble. Maybe they're right."

"And now you're painting your island," he said.

Carrie nodded. "But maybe that's some kind of symp-

122

tom, too," she said wearily. "How do I know?"

It was raining when she left the building, a cold March drizzle. Across the street the steep sides of the Prudential Building winked with lights. Traffic poured over the bridge from the Outer Drive. Carrie stopped in the entrance to tuck her folders into her book bag. Then she went down to the corner of Michigan and Randolph to catch a taxi.

Days when the weather was bad, taxis were often hard to get. Sometimes she missed the 5:30 train altogether as a result. She stood on the corner, looking up Michigan and then along Randolph. Cars whished past, making liquid sounds on the wet pavement. She hunched into her coat and shivered. Across Randolph, red neon marked the entrance to the I. T. station, and, beyond it, the Chicago Public Library crouched like an ill-tempered mastodon in the rain. The only taxis that passed were already full.

Then she saw a yellow light. That meant that an empty taxi was coming toward her in the stream of traffic. Carrie went to the edge of the curb and waved, but the taxi stopped a little farther up the block and pulled over. A couple, a man and woman, stepped off the curb. Carrie was surprised to recognize Mrs. Ramsay.

Maybe she's going to catch the 5:30, too, Carrie thought, and waved harder. We could share the taxi to the station. But the cab pulled out into the traffic again, and neither Mrs. Ramsay nor the man with her looked in Carrie's direction as they passed.

That must have been Mr. Ramsay, Carrie thought, and remembered Mrs. Ramsay's charcoal sketch. Then she saw a yellow light approaching on Randolph and began to wave again.

"You miss your train?" Sophie asked.

"I had to take the six-fifteen. I couldn't get a taxi right away." She dumped-her book bag on the kitchen table. "What smells good?"

"Leg of lamb." Sophie opened the oven to show her.

"How soon?"

"Ten minutes. Will you get that bag off the table right now!"

Carrie picked up the bag and slung it over her shoulder. Once in a while she recognized that there had been small changes since Christmas. Three months ago Sophie would have spoken to her carefully about her book bag if she'd mentioned it at all. Today she could just as well have been yelling at Duncan.

· 24 ·

Friday's drizzle had become snow overnight, and after lunch Duncan announced that he was going to build a fort in the front yard. Carrie offered to help him. "It's good snow," Duncan said as proudly as if he had created it himself. "Nice and wet so it'll pack."

He was bossy once they were outside. "Carrie, don't do

it like that. The sides have to curve in." He straightened up, red-faced from cold and exertion, and surveyed what she was doing. "If you build it straight, anybody can attack from the side—don't you know that?"

"Quiet, Duncan," Carrie said. "You didn't invent snow forts." She dug down with woolen hands and piled and dug again, through months of accumulated snowfall until she reached grass, then dug in a new spot. She felt like a dog. Her jeans were wet and her knees were numb from crawling. It was going to be an enormous fort.

Digging, piling, she thought about her drawing lesson. She was still drawing with charcoal on Saturday mornings. She felt shy about taking her watercolors to show Mrs. Ramsay, but she knew that eventually she would.

Carrie inched sideways, leaving a narrow patch of wispy yellow grass behind. It hadn't been Mrs. Ramsay in Chicago at all. She'd mentioned it this morning, and Mrs. Ramsay had said, "No." Strange, because the woman in the cab had looked just like her.

"Can't you work any faster?" Duncan yelled from his end of the fort. Carrie ignored him.

After a while she heard his voice again and looked up from her digging. He was talking to Matt Spangler. "Tomorrow," Duncan was saying, "I'm going to get out the hose and ice it. You can help build if you want. Anybody can."

Matt was standing on the front walk in his sheepskin jacket. "Can't right now," he said, "Maybe later on."

"Or you could build your own," said Duncan, "and then we could have a real snowball war—Carrie and Moira and me against you and Daniel."

"Sounds good," Matt said, "but right now I'm taking your sister over to Colby's."

Carrie sat back on her heels and watched him walk up to their front door. He rang the bell and, in a minute, Moira answered. She came out in her new green wool coat.

"What are you going over to Colby's for?" asked Duncan.

"To listen to records."

"*More* records? Boy. I'd think your ears would fall off, Moira."

Carrie brushed back her hair and pulled her cap down tighter. Moira looked nice. The coat was pretty.

"Moira's gotten completely useless," Duncan said after they'd left.

Carrie watched the two of them cut diagonally across the street. The top of Moira's head came just even with Matt's shoulder. Carrie looked down at her mittens. They were clotted with snow and mud and wisps of dead grass. More than that, they barely fit. They were a pair of little kid's mittens that stopped at her wrist.

She saw Moira's coat flash green at the corner and then disappear. With her thumb she drew a diagonal line in the snow—Moira's path. She felt somehow embarrassed to have been out there digging in the snow with Duncan in wet blue jeans and too-small mittens when Moira went off. She wondered if Moira had been embarrassed, too.

126

"Come on, Carrie," Duncan said. "You're just sitting there."

"I think I'm going to quit," she said. "I don't feel like building any more."

Duncan made a disgusted noise and said something under his breath.

"Look, I did one whole side," said Carrie. "Stop complaining." Then she stood up and brushed snow from her legs and her mittens. "Anyway," she said, "I have homework."

It was true that she had homework. She always had plenty of it, but that wasn't the reason for going inside. The reason was simply that suddenly she'd felt funny out in the snow playing games with Duncan.

She took a bath to get warm. It was a luxury to lie in the tub and not have Moira pounding to get in. Carrie poured in bath salts and took her time soaking.

She studied herself under the water. She was changing. Most of the changing had come since Christmas. It hadn't taken very long. It made her feel strange to have these things happening. It was as if her body had decided to take a direction of its own without her consent.

Irritably she pulled a washcloth off the rack and spread it over her. But that isn't going to stop it happening, she thought. Nothing is. Suddenly she wasn't enjoying the bath any more. She got out and pulled out the plug.

If, for the most part, Carrie disliked Sylvester, there
was at least one portion of the day that she loved—math
class. She loved everything about it, even the room where it
was held. She knew the room was like every other one in
the school—overheated and stuffy and furnished with the
same chalkboard and desks—but because it was the room
where she took math, it was different.

The students were different. Students who took accelerated math tended to be serious or at least serious for the
time they were in class, and, for Carrie, this made them
nicer. "Well, maybe 'nicer' isn't the right word," she said,
trying to explain the difference to Mrs. Ramsay. "It makes
them easier for me to understand—more like me, I guess."

"You see?" said Mrs. Ramsay. "I told you you'd find a
place in the puzzle that felt comfortable."

"Yes, but math only meets five times a week for fifty
minutes. That's not a very big place," said Carrie.

"It's something."

On Monday morning Carrie sat in her third-hour study
hall impatiently. She had English to read, but she didn't
want to read it. She didn't know what it was she wanted to
do.

The weather had turned balmy overnight. False spring.
Carrie looked past the heads of the other students to the
parking lot beyond the window. Weak sunlight lay on the
snow around its edges. The few remaining elms in the yard

were softening, beginning to turn pink along the branches where little leaf buds were forming. Carrie fidgeted. Maybe I have false spring fever, she thought.

The hand on the wall clock jumped forward. Carrie decided there was no point in trying to study. She would sign out and go up to math class early.

The math class door was open. A couple of kids were sitting in the room working on problems. One of them was Daniel Spangler. He smiled at her when she walked in. It really *was* a nice smile. As Moira said, Daniel was kind of funny looking, but his face had something nice about it, serious and friendly at the same time. "Did you figure out the eighth problem?" he asked.

Carrie nodded. "But it took me a long time."

"You know why?" Daniel grinned. "Because we haven't had that kind of equation yet. Herlock must have put the problem in by mistake."

"No, he showed us last week," Carrie said, "at the end of the period. He didn't explain it much."

Daniel started to flip back through the pages of his notebook. "You sure?"

"Yes. Here. If you don't have it, you can copy mine." Carrie handed him her math notes.

"Did you do that?" Daniel said. He was pointing to the margin of a page. Carrie leaned over to look. It was a tiny sketch of Mr. Herlock that she'd done in class one day.

"Yes."

"It's good. It looks a lot like him."

It did look a lot like him. Carrie was embarrassed, but she was pleased Daniel had noticed. "Sometimes I do those when I get bored," she said.

"You want to see what I can draw?" said Daniel. "Cats. That's all I can do. Cats from the back—two circles and a tail."

Carrie laughed. She watched while he drew what he'd described. "Don't you ever try drawing anything else?" she asked.

"Nope. Just cats. That's all the talent I have."

Carrie laughed again, surprising herself at how easily she laughed.

Daniel began to copy her notes. She bent down to put her books under her chair. She would have liked to keep laughing and talking. It felt easy and nice there in the math room—and funny. Nothing had seemed funny that way for ages. Maybe it means I'm better, Carrie thought.

Daniel handed back the notebook. "Has anyone asked you about the math group?" he said.

Carrie shook her head.

"It's to review for the midterm and then, later, the final—some of us from the class. I'm trying to get it organized."

"Nobody's asked me."

"Jackson was supposed to, but he never remembers anything. Anyway, do you want to?"

"When?" Carrie said.

"After school. Maybe Wednesdays and Fridays."

"I can't do it after school."

"At all? Any day?"

"No. Not any day," Carrie said flatly, and all at once the good feeling was gone.

"Oh," Daniel said. Carrie knew that she must have sounded rude. She bent down and rummaged among her books, stiff and clumsy and miserable. And then Mr. Herlock came into the room, and everyone settled down with open notebooks.

Carrie wrote the date—March 30—with her ballpoint. She looked at the cat Daniel had drawn in the margin. She was sorry she'd seemed rude. She should have told the truth—just said it right out.

She looked up at Mr. Herlock, but really she was looking beyond him at the chalkboard and, beyond that, at the office in Chicago with its digital clock and brown leather chair and water stain that reminded her of a rabbit. What if she'd told the truth? Who would understand it?

Then she saw herself as someone else would see her—skinny and awkward and shy—a person who had to go day after day to a psychiatrist because she had cracked up in the fall.

She was suddenly overwhelmed by this picture. How could she ever have considered telling people the truth? Moira was right. Her mother was right. She bent over the equation in her notebook, swallowing hard to keep from crying. She was a creep, that was all. As Duncan said, a weirdie.

The equation blurred. Carrie swallowed harder. Slowly the figures came back into focus, and she made herself listen to Mr. Herlock, but the pleasure she usually felt in math class was gone.

Across the aisle Daniel was scribbling in the margin of his notebook. Drawing cats, Carrie thought. She wondered what it would be like to be an ordinary person drawing cats. She wondered if that was something she ever could be.

◦ 26 ◦

"It's going to be really good," Duncan said. *"Space* monsters and all that."

He was hanging on her doorknob, chewing bubble gum and popping it. "Come on and go with me, Care."

"I don't like space monsters," said Carrie.

"But these are really good ones. You'll like these."

Eventually she agreed to go. "I think it's always going to be winter," she said as she slopped along beside Duncan through slush.

"Naw. It's melting."

They crossed the street. "How come you aren't going to the movies with Roger?" she asked.

"Roger? He's a creep."

"I thought he was your best friend."

"He was. Now he's David's."

"And that makes him a creep?"

Duncan gave her an exasperated look. "Don't you know anything, Carrie? If a person is your best friend and then he stops being your friend and starts being someone else's, he's a creep. Right?''

Carrie nodded. She knew that in some basic way he *was* right.

"What about people who go to psychiatrists?" she asked abruptly.

"I don't get it."

"Are they creeps?"

"You mean like you? Naw."

"Why not? I bet a lot of people think so."

"No, they don't. A person who goes to a psychiatrist—that's like someone going to a doctor."

"So?"

"So if you need your tonsils out or something, then you have to go to a doctor, that's all. It doesn't make you a creep." Duncan stopped to retrieve a large branch from the gutter.

"You're just repeating what Mother and Daddy told you," Carrie said.

"Yeah, but it's true."

Duncan stepped back onto the walk. He began pushing the branch along in front of him like a divining rod.

"But what did you think *before* they told you that?"

Duncan shrugged. "I didn't understand about a psychiatrist before that."

Carrie grinned. "You're nice, Duncan."

"Quit it."

"You are, though. I'll buy you your popcorn."

That turned out to be expensive. Duncan chose the largest

size, buttered. Then he led her into the theater. He liked sitting in the first row.

"It's full," he said in disgust. "We should have hurried."

They had to settle for the third row. It was almost full, too. They climbed in over legs and sat down and found several of Duncan's friends in the seats ahead of them.

"How come your sister's sitting with you?" Jeffrey Spencer said to Duncan.

"Why shouldn't she?"

"My sister wouldn't."

"So?" Duncan crammed a handful of popcorn into his mouth.

"Sew buttons on eggs," Jeffrey said and turned around.

Carrie looked behind her. The theater was full of fourth and fifth graders waiting for the Saturday matinee to start. Anyone older was conspicuously taller in the rows of small heads, like a weed overlooked when the grass is cut. Near the center Carrie could see several such heads sitting together and recognized them as kids from her class. She supposed they could recognize her, too, down there in the third row with Duncan and his friends. She turned around and looked at the screen. As if that were a signal, the cartoon began.

The cartoon was dumb. The main feature was terrible. After the first thirty minutes Carrie stopped paying attention and simply watched the figures moving on the screen. Duncan and his friends loved it. They commented on everything. The audience buzzed. They were watching

Laser Man scale the side of a crater.

Carrie shifted in the seat, stretched her legs sideways, and tried to be interested. Laser Man was boring through solid rock with his laser eye beam. The mountain was crumbling. Then huge green space lizards appeared, crawling toward him. Beside her, Duncan drew in his breath.

Carrie reached over and took a handful of popcorn. She figured the movie was three-quarters over. One of the lizards had Laser Man pinned on the edge of a precipice. Why didn't he just use his eye beam and crumble the thing? She glanced at Duncan. He was sitting far forward in his seat, chewing slowly.

Then something happened, but Carrie missed it. The lizard was catapulting into the chasm. The mountain was falling to dust around him. The audience cheered. Then Laser Man was kissing Cynthia. The movie was nearly over.

"Yuck," Duncan said loudly.

"Sex-ee," said Jeffrey and whistled.

The whole audience was whistling. Carrie looked at Cynthia and Laser Man standing arm in arm as the picture faded out. She began putting on her coat.

"I hate that gross stuff," Duncan said. "They always foul up the last part with junk like that."

"That's what my sister likes," Jeffrey said. "She goes to whole movies where that's all they do."

"Gross," Duncan said peacefully. He tipped up his popcorn box and emptied it into his mouth. Then he stamped on it.

"Ready?" Carrie said. They went up the aisle slowly

because they had to wait for the other forty rows to empty ahead of them.

"Wasn't it great?" said Duncan.

"That's not my favorite kind of movie."

"You like that kind Jeff was talking about, with all the kissing?"

"I don't know what kind he means exactly."

Slowly they elbowed their way through the lobby and eventually reached the street doors. It was drizzling again. "You want to get some pizza?" Duncan asked.

"After all that popcorn?"

"Just a piece."

"No," Carrie said, "I don't have any money left."

They started up Main past the already lighted storefronts. "So what kind of movies *do* you like?" Duncan said.

"Different kinds."

"The lovey ones?"

"Oh, Duncan, I don't know."

"Did you ever kiss anyone, Carrie? A boy, I mean."

"No."

"Do you want to? Jeffrey says that's all girls think about."

"Jeffrey doesn't know everything."

"Well, Roger's sister—you know her? She's going with Arthur Cox, and Roger says that's all they do—kiss, kiss."

Carrie pushed up her collar and hunched down into her jacket. "I never have."

"Roger's sister is thirteen, same as you."

"I know."

"So probably you'll start pretty soon. Moira does. I saw her and Matt once."

"Duncan, could we please stop talking about this?" Carrie said.

"What's wrong with talking about it?"

"It's not your business, for one thing." Carrie took a long breath. "And I never *have* kissed anybody. And, as Jeffrey said, his sister would never go to the movies with a bunch of fifth graders like I did. And, Duncan, I have to go to a psychiatrist every day. Nobody else does that. It makes me feel like a creep, that's all."

"Oh."

"So can we change the subject?"

"We could talk about my hockey game," Duncan said.

"Fine."

In her room Carrie turned on her desk lamp. Then she opened the closet door and looked at herself in the full-length mirror. She looked hard at her face and then at her body. There she was. Skinny, mouse-haired Carrie Stokes. That's what people saw when they looked at her.

She pressed her face against the mirror and gazed at her eyes close up. That's how it would be to kiss someone, all scrunched up face to face. Except her eyes would be closed. At least she thought they would be.

"What are you doing?" Moira was standing in the bathroom doorway.

Carrie started. "Looking at myself."

Moira came into the room. "Do you have to wear that T-shirt?" she said.

"Why not?" Carrie looked at the shirt. It was an old green one.

"Because it's about three sizes too small."

"It is?"

"Look at it."

Carrie looked into the mirror.

"Plus it's too tight."

"Tight how?"

"God, Carrie, don't you notice *anything?* Look at yourself."

Again Carrie looked.

"You can't go around like that. You're not a little kid."

Carrie folded her arms across her chest. "What're you talking about?"

"You know perfectly well what I'm talking about. You ought to be wearing a bra."

"I don't have a bra."

"Well, they sell them right down in the Village."

Carrie sat down and kicked the closet door shut. "Why don't you mind your own business, Moira?"

Moira shrugged. "Okay," she said. "Do what you want." Then she went back into her own room. In a minute Carrie heard her stereo go on.

With the toe of her sneaker Carrie nudged the closet door open again. Then she pulled up her shirt and looked at herself. She'd known it was happening, of course, but she hadn't thought it showed. After a few minutes she got up and put on a sweater.

"I am getting breasts," she said, staring hard at the ceiling.

"How do you feel about that?" His voice sounded exactly as it always did, but Carrie couldn't look at him.

"I wish I wasn't."

"Why?"

"I'm scared."

Next he would ask what scared her and she would not be able to explain. And so she stared steadfastly at the ceiling and told him, instead, about things that happened Saturday.

After a while she had gone into Moira's room. "I'm sorry I was crabby. There are just some things I don't like to talk about."

"Yeah, I know."

Moira was filing her nails. She reached over and turned down the music.

"I need to ask you something," Carrie said. "But you have to promise you won't laugh. Okay?"

Moira nodded.

"Promise," Carrie said.

"I promise I won't laugh."

"All right then." Carrie hesitated. "Moira, you know when you kiss somebody—" She hesitated again, and Moira nodded encouragingly. "Well, how do you breathe?"

"You're kidding!" Moira dropped the emery board and simply stared. "You can't be serious."

"You promised you wouldn't laugh."

"I'm not laughing, but breathe! I don't know how you breathe! You just do. That's the weirdest question I ever heard."

"Do you kiss Matt?" Carrie went on doggedly.

"Some. Sure."

"Does it scare you?"

"No."

"But did it ever?"

Moira looked thoughtful. "I guess maybe a little a long time ago."

Carrie squatted down on the floor and began to twist a loop of carpet between her fingers. "Nothing's hard for you, is it?" she said.

"Math. That's impossible."

"But this kind of stuff. For you it's easy. For me it isn't. I wonder why we're different."

Moira picked up the emery board and began filing again. "This 'stuff,' Carrie—that's all just natural."

"I know."

"It's nothing to be scared of. It just happens. You can't help it happening."

Carrie looked up from the loop she was twisting. "Moira," she said, "about the bra—I'm embarrassed to ask Mother and I'm embarrassed to go in and buy one. Would you buy it for me?"

"Sure." Moira smiled at her.

"I don't really want one, but if you think I should—"

Carrie watched her sister smoothing her nail. She felt she had other, harder questions to ask but no words to ask them. Finally she said softly, "Moira, don't you still kind of believe in the fish language—even though you're older now?"

"No. I tell you that every time you ask."

"Did you stop a very long time ago?"

"Ages ago."

Carrie felt questions struggling inside her. She didn't know how to ask them. She leaned forward. Her voice became urgent, too high.

"Do *I* have to stop, Moira?" she cried. "Do I *have* to?"

Moira looked at her. "You *know* it was a game," Moira said.

"But I want to believe it! I don't want to lose everything!"

"Lose what?" Moira said. "What do you mean by everything?"

Carrie drew in her breath and shook her head, "I can't explain."

Moira leaned forward and ruffled Carrie's hair. It was an unusual thing for her to do, something she hadn't done since they were children. "It'll be all right," she said.

Then she got up and opened a bureau drawer and began sorting through her stacked sweaters. "You know, Carrie," she said, "sometimes—when you're talking about math or art or something—you sound like you're about twenty-five Other times—now, for instance—you sound like a baby. I don't understand what makes the difference."

"I don't know why you would understand," Carrie said quietly. "I don't understand much about it myself."

Moira pulled out a gray slipover and held it up to inspect it.

"Are you going out?" Carrie said.

"After dinner."

"Will you get me the bra on Monday?"

"Yes. Sure I will. In fact what I'll do is get you a couple of them." Then Moira went into the bathroom and turned on the shower.

After dinner Carrie tried watching television with Duncan, but the programs he chose bored her. She went into her room and got out her paints.

She filled a glass with water, spread newspaper on the desk, and opened her watercolor pad. She dipped her brush and began a blue wash, stroking the color gently onto the white paper. She could hear Duncan snort with amusement from time to time and a steady drone of voices from the program.

She lay a wash of deeper blue onto the original strokes of color. She imagined a blue sea, many shades of blue, carrying her on its current as she painted it. But the noises from Duncan's room kept distracting her. She got up and closed the door.

Ordinarily nothing distracted her when she was painting. Once she began, the colors seemed to sweep her out beyond the desk and the room and the noises around her, and she felt almost as though she had entered the picture itself, like a traveler crossing the border between two countries. But tonight was different.

She looked at what she had done. It bored her. She supposed that what she had begun would turn out to be another view of the island. She didn't feel like painting the island. She licked the tip of her brush, doodled a design on the paper's margin, and considered packing up the paints.

Then, timidly, she began enlarging the design, starting a border of leaves and vines around the paper. She added squirrels scampering on branches, a few birds and a mouse. Then faces. She drew little figures climbing the vines, faces peeping from between leaves. She doodled in Mr. Herlock. She did a figure of Sophie from the rear. She was so absorbed that when Duncan opened the door she didn't hear him.

"Want a Coke?" he said.

Carrie looked up.

"What're you drawing?"

"Nothing really, just doodling."

Duncan came in and looked over her shoulder.

"Hey, that's good," he said. "Look at all the people you've got in there—Sophie and Jeffrey and that guy that cut our grass last summer."

"You're seeing things. Those are just faces."

"They look like those people to me."

Carrie studied the border. She had covered almost all four edges of the paper.

"So do you want a Coke?" Duncan asked again.

"Not right now."

She wanted to finish what she was doing. In the gap that was left she drew a little figure of Duncan on hockey skates, and then, to finish it, she drew a cat like Daniel's—two circles and a tail—and sat him on the curly tendril of a vine.

·28·

Finally, in the middle of April, the last of the winter's snow began to disappear. The gutters ran with water, and Carrie could smell something like spring in the air.

She inhaled a deep breath of it. "I'll bet there are some crocuses in Mrs. Padmore's yard," she said to Moira on the way to school.

"What made you think of that?" said Moira.

"I was just remembering how we used to go over and look at them."

"You should stop calling it Mrs. Padmore's," Moira said. "The Spanglers have been there since before Christmas."

Carrie inhaled again and ignored Moira. She had a quiz in English first hour. She thought about that.

A few blocks from Sylvester the Spanglers caught up with them. "Slowpokes," Moira said.

"Because of Daniel," said Matt. "He couldn't find his history paper."

144

Daniel fell into step beside Carrie. "I forgot I left it in the bathroom," he said.

"The Caesar paper?" said Carrie, and then, because it was on her mind, "Are the crocuses up in your yard, did you notice?"

As soon as she'd said it she felt silly, but Daniel didn't laugh. "I don't know what crocuses look like," he said.

They started up the driveway to school. "Are you still busy every afternoon?" said Daniel. "The math group's meeting Wednesdays."

"I still am," Carrie said softly and looked down at her boots and couldn't think of anything more to say until they'd reached the doors.

Inside they all headed for their lockers. Carrie slipped off her coat as she went.

"Carrie!" someone called behind her.

She turned. Katherine Fowles was hurrying to catch up.

"Did you study for the quiz?"

"Last night."

"Well, look, I didn't have a chance to." Katherine drew up beside her, out of breath. "Something came up and I couldn't study."

Carrie waited.

"What I was wondering," Katherine said, "I mean, you know the way we sit in English class? If you just turned your paper a little bit, I could get a look at it. I don't mean copy or cheat or anything like that. I mean just kind of help my memory a little bit."

"Why don't you ask Mrs. Gordon if you can take the quiz tomorrow?" Carrie said.

"She'd never let me."

"Sure she would. She's nice about things like that. She let me make up a lot of work after Christmas."

"I know she wouldn't let *me*. I had to ask her once last week, because I got behind then, too."

Carrie glanced sideways at Katherine. She didn't feel sorry for her. "Well, I'm not going to let you copy from me," she said.

"I didn't say copy. I said help my memory is all."

Carrie shook her head. "Ask Mrs. Gordon."

"Maybe she'll let *you* make up quizzes. We all know *you're* special."

"What do you mean?"

"Nothing."

"What?" Carrie persisted.

"Well, we all know there's something wrong with you. That's why the teachers go easy on you."

"That's a lie," Carrie said. "Nobody goes easy on me."

"That's your opinion."

They'd reached Carrie's locker. Carrie turned to Katherine. "What do you think is wrong with me?"

Katherine shrugged. "Who knows? Something, though, ever since your so-called bronchitis."

"Like what?" Carrie said. "*Why* do you think there's anything wrong?"

Katherine regarded her with her little raisin-hole eyes.

"Well, isn't there?" she said. "I've always thought so. How come you don't go to the dances? How come you don't have any friends? How come you always go off by yourself after school?"

Carrie stopped short. Katherine's face bobbed like a white balloon in front of her. She clutched the strap of her book bag and looked into Katherine's stupid little eyes. She wanted to kill her.

"Well, how come?" said Katherine.

Carrie took a deep breath. "You don't know anything, Katherine," she said.

Katherine shrugged and turned away. "Anyway, thanks for nothing," she called.

Carrie stood still beside her locker while people hurried past. She heard the bell for morning assembly ring and didn't move. She would not stay. She would miss the quiz. She didn't care. Slowly she turned and started toward the front door.

But halfway there she stopped. Anger made a hard little knot in her chest. She turned and ran back down the hall and, dodging between the crowds, headed for Mr. Adderley's office. She wouldn't be a creep any more if that's what everyone thought.

Mr. Adderley's secretary was sitting at her desk with a mug of coffee. The mug said "Good Morning" in orange letters.

"You're going to be late," she said to Carrie.

"I know but I have to ask you something."

Carrie rested both palms on the desk and caught her breath. "You know I paid you in November for those dances?"

"Sure. I remember. You weren't feeling well."

"And then I got sick and I never went to any."

Mr. Adderley's secretary nodded above the steam from her cup.

"Well, can I still go? Am I still signed up?"

"I think so. There's only one dance left this spring, but I don't see why you can't go to it."

"Okay," Carrie said. "That's what I wanted to know." And then she hoisted her book bag and ran for her locker.

Morning assembly was over and the bell for first hour was ringing by the time she'd hung up her coat. Carrie grabbed her books and ran up the stairs to English class. She slid into the seat behind Katherine and dumped her things under it. Mrs. Gordon was already passing out the quiz questions.

Carrie sat staring at Katherine's wide back. She hoped Katherine would flunk. She hoped she would fall down the stairs and break her legs after class. She hoped Katherine would get a terrible disease that would make her hair fall out. She sat contentedly thinking these things until Mrs. Gordon reached her desk with a copy of the questions.

It wasn't until after she'd finished the quiz and handed it back that she began thinking about what she had done that morning. I can change my mind, she thought. I don't have to go. She knew that the last dance wasn't until the first part of June, and that gave her plenty of time to think about it.

"I finally brought you my watercolors," Carrie said on Saturday morning. "But I'm kind of scared to show them to you."

"Why scared?" Mrs. Ramsay was halfway through the kitchen doorway with a cereal bowl in one hand.

"Well, what if you don't like them?"

"What if I don't?"

The remains of the children's breakfast were strewn across the table in the dining room. "Want help?" Carrie asked and picked up a plate without waiting for an answer.

The house was more chaotic than ever. On the table a milk-drowned bowl of cereal shared space with a flashlight, a sock, and the Ramsays' cat. "If you'll hand me that bowl, then the cat will move and we'll make some space," Mrs. Ramsay said. She looked tired, Carrie thought, and she seemed thinner.

Carrie picked her way to the kitchen sink through a maze of Lego bits and crayons and discarded clothes and tried to find a place to dump the cereal. Dinner dishes still crowded the sink. A frying pan rimmed with congealed fat sat on top. "Everything's a mess," Mrs. Ramsay said. "I apologize." She said it wearily.

"Do you feel all right today?" Carrie looked at her. "We can wait until next week if you'd rather."

"No. I'm tired, but I want to see the watercolors. And as a matter of fact, we can't wait until next week, if you're thinking of entering any of them. Entries close Friday."

So Carrie opened the folder and spread the pictures out on the cleanest end of the dining room table, separating them into two groups. Mrs. Ramsay dumped cereal, ran water, and came back with a cloth to mop the table.

"Oh, Carrie!" she said, pausing with the cloth in midair. "Oh, Carrie!"

"What do you think?"

"Well." And then she stopped and really began to look at the pictures. Carrie watched apprehensively as she lifted each one, held it at arm's length, lifted another. "Well," she finally said, "I think it's the best work you've ever done."

Carrie sat down hard on a dining room chair. "Really?" And suddenly her throat ached.

"Absolutely."

"I was so afraid they weren't any good," she said.

"Actually they're pretty wonderful."

Mrs. Ramsay took the stacks of pictures into the living room. With a foot, she moved cups and magazines and toys aside, making room, and then she lay the pictures side by side on the floor, almost tenderly.

"Choosing only twelve will be hard."

"I did that," Carrie said. "That first stack has the best ones, I think."

Mrs. Ramsay continued to look, walking up and down the rows of pictures like someone studying sidewalk painting. Once in a while she squatted to look at a picture closely with thumbs hooked in the back pockets of her jeans.

Carrie waited. She was filled with relief.

"I can tell you I wish that *I'd* painted them," Mrs. Ramsay said at last. "You must be very proud."

"Really I wasn't anything until now," Carrie said. "I just painted. I couldn't tell if the pictures were good. I mean, I couldn't trust that they were until you'd seen them."

"You suspected, I'll bet."

"A little."

Mrs. Ramsay flopped onto a corner of the sofa, pulled a package of cigarettes from her pocket, and lit one.

"What about all the pictures having the same subject?" Carrie said. "Is that all right?"

Mrs. Ramsay shrugged. "Why not? Look at Monet's haystacks. After all," she said, "the pictures aren't the same, Carrie. They are one subject painted many ways."

"I guess."

"That island must mean a lot to you."

Carrie was sitting on the floor. She stretched out her legs and let the cat crawl into her lap. "It does."

And then they spent most of an hour on their knees crawling among the pictures and choosing while the cat lay on the sofa giving himself a bath.

It was noon before they finished. Carrie looked at the final choices spread out apart from the others and felt well satisfied. Mrs. Ramsay had seen what she hadn't, that these twelve pictures—all of them views of the island's headland—formed a kind of progression. In each successive picture the details grew clearer. It was as if the cliffs were slowly emerging from mist, as if morning sun were burning off a haze.

"Mrs. Ramsay," she said, sitting back on her heels, "I'm excited."

"You ought to be. So am I."

The cat leaped delicately from the table into Mrs. Ramsay's lap and settled. She scratched between his ears.

"I don't think I'll be painting the island much more, though," Carrie said. "The other night I began another picture of it, but I couldn't get into it. I ended up drawing figures and faces."

"You've gone through several things this year, haven't you?" Mrs. Ramsay said. "Abstractions and then these lovely watercolors. So why not figures? Maybe figures and faces will be next, and I'll want to see those, too."

She kept scratching the cat absently, looking toward the window where sun was struggling its way between clouds. "I'll enter the pictures the first of the week," she said, "but there won't be word until September."

"That's okay," Carrie said lightly. "I'm getting to be very patient."

She felt full of lightness, light as a soap bubble. She was happy about the pictures. She was happy Mrs. Ramsay liked them. "I can wait a year," she said, but saw that Mrs. Ramsay wasn't listening. She was gazing out the window, still scratching the cat. Her face looked very tired.

"Carrie," she said, "when the results do come, I very

likely won't be here. I won't be teaching next year at Sylvester."

Carrie looked at her questioningly, feeling the bubble begin to lose air. "Where will you be?"

"After school's over—sometime this summer—the children and I will be moving away."

"Oh." Carrie picked up a red crayon from the floor and turned it slowly between her fingers. "Did Mr. Ramsay get transferred?" she said. That happened a lot to people in Northpoint.

"No. He's staying here. It's only the children and I who are leaving. Mr. Ramsay and I won't be living together any more."

Carrie sat back and hugged her knees. "Oh." Then after a minute, "Do you mean you're going to get divorced?"

"Yes, probably. My parents live in Milwaukee. We'll go there for a while and then see."

The cat stood up and arched his back and yawned. Carrie reached out, and he came padding softly into her arms. "Milwaukee's pretty close," she said finally.

"Very close."

Carrie hugged the cat to her chest, feeling the warmth of his fur. "I'm sorry," she said.

Mrs. Ramsay nodded.

"I'll miss you," Carrie said softly and then bent her face into the cat's warm coat.

"Carrie, look—" Mrs. Ramsay began and paused as if she were trying to find a way to say something hard. "It's what I want to do," she finished. "I think it will be all right."

There was noise on the front porch, a clatter, and then Saskia's voice yelling at her brother. Carrie released the cat. "Lots of people go to Milwaukee, even just for the day," she said.

"Sure they do. You can come up there to see me."

After a while Carrie began to collect her pictures, and Mrs. Ramsay helped, keeping aside the dozen they had decided to enter. Carrie couldn't think of anything more to say, and they finished gathering the pictures in silence.

Saskia was alone on the front walk when Carrie left the house. She was pushing herself along on one roller skate. "Pretty soon I'm going to skate on two," she said, "when this one foot gets good at it."

"It's easier to learn on two," Carrie said. "Really. If you put on the other one, I'll pull you to the corner."

Saskia looked doubtful, but she sat down and fastened on the other skate.

Carrie helped her stand up and then steadied her. "Hold on to me," she said.

Saskia wavered forward and gripped Carrie's waist. "Don't go fast."

They went up the street slowly, with Saskia clutching Carrie's coat and the skates whirring on the concrete. Carrie remembered doing the very same thing with Moira, only then it had been Moira pulling her. Saskia tugged at her waist. "Slow down!"

Carrie looked around. "You're all right."

"How'm I going to get back?"

"Well, you could take off one skate, but why don't you try it on two? You've got to be brave."

Saskia stood uncertainly, with her tongue between her teeth. "You watch me then."

Carrie stood at the top of the street and watched her, arms windmilling, coast down the sidewalk. She didn't fall. She grew smaller and smaller and, when she reached her own walk, she waved.

Carried smiled. By summertime Saskia would be skating all over the place. But summer was months away. It would be months before the Ramsays left. Carrie didn't have to think about it yet.

◊ 30 ◊

In May the crabapple trees began to bloom. Whole streets in Northpoint exploded into pink clouds of blossom, and the strange damp odor of the flowers was everywhere. They bloomed, then faded, and petals drifted in the gutters.

On the first Friday morning in June Carrie announced at breakfast that she was going to go to the junior dance that night.

Her mother put down the cup she was holding. "What are you going to wear?" she said.

"There's that dress we bought at Saks."

155

"It's wool."

"I'll find something. I can borrow from Moira."

Moira looked up from buttering her toast and said, "Let her do it her own way, Mother."

Carrie had not tried to imagine what it would be like. She knew it was something she needed to do, and so she was going to do it. That evening her father drove her to the club in Moira's dress. "I'll bet you'll have yourself a great time," he said. And Carrie didn't disagree, because there was no use trying to explain that it wasn't a good time she was going there for.

"You call when you want a ride home."

"I will," she said, sitting with her hands clasped tight in her lap as they drove up to the entrance behind half a dozen other cars.

She followed a group of girls from school into the ballroom. A record was playing. The French doors stood open, and Carrie thought for a moment of dashing across the gleaming floor and out through the doors and hiding until it was over. But she had decided to come, she thought, and now she would stay.

Mrs. Mitchell was just as Moira had described her. She was small and plump. Her hair was dyed black, and she wore very high heels. Carrie looked at her and at the kids straggling in through the doors, joining into groups and laughing. She recognized them all. Nobody commented on her being there. Nobody noticed. She stood by herself against the wall and watched as if she were watching a play.

She saw Katherine Fowles come in in a dress that made

156

her look fatter and whiter and more loathsome than ever. She saw Daniel. She realized that what Moira said was true. Everyone in eighth grade came to the dances.

The record changed, became a march. Mrs. Mitchell began calling them to line up for a Grand-Right-and-Left. Carrie joined them. It was like a square dance. She moved from hand to hand in time with the music, passing one eighth-grade boy after another until, all at once, the record stopped. "Take your partners for the foxtrot," Mrs. Mitchell called, and Carrie found she was face-to-face with a boy from her history class. He took her hand and put his arm around her waist. They danced.

Carrie had no idea what to do, but she tried to move in the way he was moving. Neither of them spoke. Around them other couples danced, arms pumping. Some chattered. Others danced in silence, as Carrie and her partner were doing. Then, "How long do we do this?" Carrie asked.

"Until the end of the record. Then you change partners."

The record ended, and they changed, and Carrie danced with another boy as silently as she had with the first. And then with another. The dances changed, too. They did several different ones, but they were all strange to her. Sometimes she glimpsed Katherine's fat rose-colored back in the crowd or Daniel's head between the dancers. She was hot. Her hand was slippery in her partner's, and the small of her back ached where he held her. "One more record till they serve punch," her partner said. "I hope it's better than what we had last time."

Carrie nodded and disengaged her hand for a moment to

brush back her hair. She thought the dance must be almost half over. She'd never have to do it again. She'd done it. She'd proved to herself that she could.

The record ended. Her partner dropped her arm and disappeared toward the punch bowl at the far end of the ballroom. Carrie wiped her hands on her skirt. Then, because she was hot, she went to stand beside one of the open French doors.

It was almost dark. Beyond the golf course she could see the lights of houses floating in the twilight like ships moored in a green harbor. She went out onto the grass and stood for a few minutes to enjoy the strangeness of it, almost forgetting what she'd been doing. But then in what seemed like no time at all, the music began again, and reluctantly she turned back toward the dancing.

There was no Grand-Right-and-Left this time. The boys chose partners. The girls left over chose each other. Nobody chose Carrie. That was all right. She stood near the door and knew she was inconspicuous. In another hour it would be over and she could go home, and she would have been at a junior dance like any other normal kid in Northpoint.

During the second hour, just as Moira had said, the kids could dance as they pleased. They liked that better. The music was different. The room grew noisy. Carrie watched them curiously. After a while she saw Daniel coming toward her. He grinned and seemed both happy and surprised to see her.

"It's really hot in here," he said.

"It is."

He flapped his jacket like wings in the open doorway. "I've only worn this coat three times," he said, "always here." And then he sneezed. "I've got an allergy."

"To what?" Carrie said.

"Some kind of pollen. I'm having tests to find out."

"Are they putting those scratches on your back?"

He nodded.

"I had those, too."

Then they were silent. Carrie looked at the dancers. Daniel continued flapping his jacket, but more slowly.

After a while he said, "Do you want to dance?"

"I don't know how very well."

"Yeah, I don't either." He seemed relieved.

"How much longer does this party go on?" Carrie asked.

"Another twenty minutes. I was thinking about leaving. Are you walking? Want to go now?"

"Okay."

"It isn't far if we cut across the golf course."

They cut across the eleventh fairway toward the lighted houses beyond. It was dark. June bugs rasped, fell silent, and then began to rasp again when they'd passed.

"Are you ready for finals?" Daniel said.

"I guess so."

"It's too bad you can't come to the math group. It's good."

"I've heard people in class say that."

They had reached the edge of the golf course. They crawled over the fence dividing it from the street and turned down Ashcroft.

"Duncan broke his arm," Carrie said.

"I saw his cast."

"He likes your guinea pig."

"I know. He always wants to see it."

"Why do you call it Guinea? Why don't you give it a name?"

"We never could think of a name. I wanted to call him Snowball, but Matt said that was stupid."

"Snowball? I think that's nice."

"I didn't mean the winter kind. I meant those big round flowers, you know? The white ones? We had a bush of them where we used to live in Virginia."

"Oh."

"Anyway—" Daniel sneezed again. "Duncan broke his arm at Little League, right?"

"Yes." Carrie said.

"I guess they have Little Leagues everywhere. We had one in Virginia."

"Did you play?"

"I did for a while. Then I quit."

"Didn't you like it or what?"

"I wasn't any good. It was Tee-League. You know, the league for the little kids?"

Carrie nodded in the darkness.

"Well, I never could get the ball to balance on the tee. I'd try and I'd get so frustrated and I'd know all the kids were standing there waiting. So one day—I don't know—I just started crying. The other kids began to laugh. Well, I ran home. I ran right off the field and went home. My father didn't make me go back. I think he was embarrassed."

Their own street was just ahead. "So, anyway," Daniel said, "that was a while ago."

They turned into the street. Carrie could see her porch light. "Did you mind moving from Virginia?" she asked.

"Some. It was lonely here at first. Sometimes I'd dream I was back home."

"I didn't like it when we moved, either," Carrie said. "I used to wish I could find a place I could stay, where nothing ever changed."

Daniel chuckled. "That'd be good, wouldn't it?"

Carrie watched him start up his driveway. He turned to wave, and his face looked nice—funny and nice—in the light from the porch. She took a step forward. "Daniel?" He stopped. "I want to tell you why I don't come to math group."

He waited.

"It isn't because I don't want to. It's because I go to see a psychiatrist every day after school."

"Oh."

He stood, it seemed to Carrie, awkwardly, waiting for her to say something more, or, perhaps, trying to think of what to answer.

"I just wanted to tell you."

He nodded. "Well," he said, "I could come over Saturdays and fill you in. Or do you go Saturdays, too?"

"No, not Saturdays. That would be nice." And then Daniel turned and went up the driveway and Carrie crossed over to her house.

She paused a minute before going in, then stooped to take off her shoes. She stepped onto the damp grass. Overhead a searchlight moved across the sky and lost itself in the branches of the maple. Carrie curled her toes in the grass and uncurled them.

She walked slowly around to the back of the house, where June bugs were whirring in the lilac bushes beyond the fish pond. The catalpa was in bloom. She sat down under it and leaned against the trunk.

Her mother said it was a messy tree, dropping all over the grass, but Carrie liked it. She ran her fingers through the fallen blossoms around her. They were wet as the grass and the texture of skin.

◦**31**◦

Then suddenly it was the first week of summer. As if on signal, on the last day of school the weather turned hot. All day sprinklers swept the lawns in Northpoint, and afternoons Carrie sweltered waiting for the 3:30 into Chicago.

Moira was working half time at the Yarn Shop. The Wednesday after school was out, Carrie went down to the Recreation Center to apply for a part-time job in the summer program.

"You want to spend all summer playing kick ball with a bunch of third graders?" Duncan asked her.

"What's wrong with that?" said Carrie.

"Big thrill."

Duncan had suddenly begun acting like a very big deal. Carrie tried to ignore him. It was either ignore him or punch him, she thought.

She didn't care what he said—she liked the summer program. Mornings she and little Sara Meyers from next door walked the six blocks to the Recreation Center together. At noon they walked home. In between there were games or field trips and, rainy mornings, miles of plastic cord to be braided into lanyards.

Sara liked to hold Carrie's hand as they walked. She liked asking questions. "How big are gorilla babies?" she would ask, damp hand gripping Carrie's. "Giant size, do you think? Or medium?" She almost never asked anything Carrie could answer.

The summer days assumed a pleasant rhythm. Mornings there was the job, then lunch. Usually after lunch Carrie painted. In late June Daniel bought a guitar. He brought it over to show her, and sometimes when she took her paints out into the yard in the afternoon she could hear him practicing.

One weekend her father decided to plant roses along the sunny side of the screened porch. Carrie helped him settle the bushes into the holes he'd dug. There were eight of them, and it took a long time.

"Does that boy know anything but 'The Blue Tail Fly'?" her father said suddenly.

163

Carrie was startled. She'd grown as used to "The Blue Tail Fly" as to hearing the whish of sprinklers. "He's just learning," she said.

"Which is he? The one Moira goes out with or the other one?"

"It's Daniel. He's the one my age."

Her father grunted and began working another rosebush out of its paper pot. Carrie listened critically for a moment. Daniel was improving.

"By next summer these bushes should be nice," her father said. "They'll be very pretty."

"Daddy," Carrie said all at once, "am *I* pretty?"

He looked at her blankly. "Sure you are," he said. "You and Moira were always pretty little girls."

"But am *I* *pretty*?" Carrie said as if he hadn't answered the question.

He smiled and patted her arm. "Pretty and getting prettier," he said. He left a streak of mud on the sleeve of her T-shirt.

The first week of July it was ninety degrees every day. Carrie watered the new rosebushes. She and Duncan played a little tennis. She painted. A flute player began practicing somewhere in the neighborhood, so that now when Carrie painted outside there were two of them to listen to. She felt as if all of them—herself and Daniel and the invisible flutist—were part of the summer afternoons in the way that bees and dragonflies were a part. It seemed to her that the music and the sunlight and the hot green stillness of the garden entered into what she was painting. Sometimes she stopped and put down her brush and realized that just then, at that moment, she was entirely happy.

She mentioned this tentatively to Dr. Ross. "I think I'm getting better. I think that now I really am." He smiled and, since he didn't smile often, she thought it must mean he agreed.

"I feel I'm getting better, but I still don't know what made me sick," she said. "Sometimes I wonder why it happened to *me*. Not to Moira, you know, or to somebody else."

She now knew better than to expect an answer. Instead there came the inevitable question. "Well, tell me, Carrie, what do you think?"

"I don't know. I think of all the people who have really terrible lives but don't do what I did. Compared to them, my life has been easy. It's always been easy."

"But not easy for you."

"Is that an answer?" Carrie said. "It sounds like a cop-out."

She frowned, listening to the hum of his air conditioner. "I'll think about it while you're away."

He would be away the whole month of August. When he'd first told her that, she had felt afraid, but slowly she'd gotten used to the idea. "I'm going to miss you," Carrie said, "but I won't miss the train trips, and it'll be kind of nice to have whole afternoons at home."

Dr. Ross smiled. Twice in one day! Then he untangled his long legs and started to stand up. The hour was over. But Carrie sat still because there was one more thing she wanted to say. "I'm not scared about it any more, though," she said. "I think I'll be all right."

He held the door for her. She walked down the hall to the elevator. She was pretty sure that what she'd said was true—at least for the month of August she could get along all right all by herself.

◦32◦

Late one August afternoon Duncan persuaded her to go out to the club to hit balls. It was really too hot. It had been hot for weeks. Even though they were constantly watered, the lawns along the way were drying up. Carrie's racket clattered in her bike basket. She pedaled lazily. It was too hot to make much effort. They coasted down the gravel slope to the courts, brakes squeaking, and could see before they got there that the courts were full.

"Darn," Duncan said.

"Somebody'll quit before long."

"There're people waiting."

"Two people."

Two girls from Moira's class, actually. Carrie tried to think of their names.

"You waiting for a court?" Duncan asked.

One of the girls nodded. "But there are a couple of courts where they're almost through."

Duncan went to get an orange soda. Carrie sat down to wait.

"So anyway," the girl said, turning back to her friend, "she's going off with some man. That's what my mother said."

"How does your mother know that?"

"My mother knows everything about everybody. Minding other people's business is her lifework."

Carrie leaned back on her elbows in the grass and watched the doubles game in front of her. They were good players. Beyond them some not-so-good players were plinking a ball back and forth in high, soft arcs. Carrie picked a clover and then another and began to braid a chain. After a few minutes this reminded her too much of doing lanyards and she stopped. She watched the doubles game again, watched a lob rise and fall short. The other player smashed it back—a nice overhead.

"So that's why she's going away." The girls on the bench were still talking. "She's going to Milwaukee because of this guy."

"Who's going to teach art? Do you know?"

Carrie turned and looked at the two of them. They were talking about Mrs. Ramsay.

"No, but my mother says they'd never keep her at Sylvester now even if she wasn't moving."

"Sure they would. Remember when Ritter got a divorce?"

"That was different. Mrs. Ritter's husband left *her*."

"So?"

"So that's different. That wasn't Mrs. Ritter's *fault*. This is like, you know, a scandal. At least that's what my mother calls it."

Carrie looked away and pretended to be watching the tennis game so the girls wouldn't know she was listening. She waited for them to say something more, but instead they began talking about a friend in Charlevoix. Then a court was free and they got up to go.

Carrie watched them walking away. She didn't understand. How could what they'd said be true? She got up and went to find Duncan. All at once she didn't want to play.

"Would you care if we didn't?"

"We rode all the way out here!"

"I know, but I feel funny, Dunc. You can find someone else who'll hit with you."

She pushed her bicycle up the hill and out onto the gravel road. Then, riding slowly, she began trying to sort out what she'd heard. She was baffled.

She pictured Mrs. Ramsay as she looked every Saturday morning, dressed in jeans and sneakers in the sunny clutter of her living room. What did any of this have to do with that? Carrie couldn't make it fit.

The weeds along the road edge looked dusty and tired. Carrie brushed against them, pedaling slowly. The girls were wrong. That had to be the answer. Somehow they'd mixed up two stories and they were really talking about someone else. One of these days she'd tell Mrs. Ramsay. They'd laugh at it together.

She could imagine doing it. They'd be standing in the kitchen waiting for water to boil, and she'd say, "Guess what stupid thing I heard?" Mrs. Ramsay would say, "Tell me." Then she'd sputter. Then they'd laugh.

Carrie smiled. She coasted onto the smooth pavement beyond the gravel. I'll ride down there now, she thought, and get it straightened out before I fuss any more. It would be simple. It would all be fine.

But she didn't do it. Instead of heading for Mrs. Ramsay's she turned toward home.

She propped her bicycle in the garage, dropped her racket on the back steps, and walked across the lawn to the fish pond. She could hear the sound of the flute coming from the next street. Its notes scattered like drops of water in the warm air. She stretched out beside the pond.

A fish swam close to the surface and darted away. Carrie reached down and stirred the water with her fingertips. There couldn't be a scandal. The rumor wasn't true. There was nothing about Mrs. Ramsay that could make it true. Carrie stirred, idly watching the fish flash deep in the water. So why not go down to her house and ask her? Carrie didn't know why not, but she didn't want to go.

She didn't go the next day, either, or any day the rest of the week. A dozen times she almost set out and each time decided not to.

·33·

Friday morning she woke exhausted. Although it was still early, the air was already thick and hot and the curtains were limp at the open window. Carrie sat up. She felt as heavy as the air. Immediately she began to think of Mrs. Ramsay. She leaned back wearily against her pillow. She was sick of thinking.

The rumor had become isolated words in her head, repeated so often that all the meaning had leaked out. Scandal. Some man. Gibberish words. She wanted to pull them out of her mind like weeds.

She closed her eyes. Sometimes if she imagined Mrs. Ramsay doing something familiar—squinting at a drawing, pouring tea—the rumor dissolved. She tried it. She imagined Mrs. Ramsay bending thoughtfully over a picture on her dining-room table. But it didn't work. She couldn't hold the image steady against the troublesome words, and they swarmed in. The image began to stretch and lose shape. And then suddenly she saw another image—a taxi passing in a cold March drizzle.

Carrie sat up straight. She stared at the wall above her desk. The taxi on Michigan Avenue. The woman who had looked like Mrs. Ramsay. Carrie drew her breath in sharply. It *had* been Mrs. Ramsay, after all. With a kind of dull certainty she knew that it had, and then all the bits of the rumor clattered into place. The man in the taxi had not been her husband. The rumor was true. Mrs. Ramsay had lied.

Carrie put her feet on the floor. She began to tremble. The silly pink bouquets on the wallpaper whirled. Mrs. Ramsay had lied to her. For months she'd been lying. Why? She could have explained to Carrie. She could have trusted Carrie to understand. They were friends, weren't they? Hadn't they been?

Anger rose like water boiling inside her. She grabbed the pillow from the bed and slammed it across the room at the desk.

The lamp tilted, rocked, crashed to the floor. The shade crumpled like a wad of paper. Stupidly Carrie watched the pillow slump sideways and tumble. The lamp was in pieces. She stared at the mess.

After a while she stood up and pulled on a pair of shorts. The knowledge was a thick pain at the bottom of her stomach. When she had finished dressing, she knelt down and began collecting pieces of the lamp.

The cord hung limp and useless, still attached to the wall. Carrie unplugged it. She loaded everything into her wastebasket, and then, wearily, she carried it downstairs.

Her mother was in the downstairs hall plucking dead leaves off a philodendron. "I broke my lamp," Carrie said.

"Oh, that pretty lamp!" her mother exclaimed. "We chose that especially to go with your wallpaper. I wonder if Mrs. Gooch can replace it."

As if the lamp had died, Carrie thought. As if a broken lamp were a terrible tragedy. How was it that in this house a broken lamp was tragic? How could that be so important to her mother?

She carried the wastebasket out to the garage and dumped the contents into a trash can. Suddenly she thought with longing of the shabby lamps and worn rugs at the Ramsays'. And then, without thinking about what she would say, or even why she was doing it, she wheeled her bike out to the street and headed for their house.

Noah and Saskia were playing on the front porch. "Want to see our caterpillar?" Noah said. "We're taking him to Milwaukee."

Carrie looked into the glass jar Noah held out to her. Buried under a handful of grass was a small caterpillar. "When are you going to Milwaukee?" she said.

"I don't know. Mom's in the kitchen packing things."

Mrs. Ramsay was wrapping plates in newspaper when Carrie walked in. "Oh, Carrie, I'm glad you came. The movers are coming tomorrow. I was going to stop by later to say good-bye."

Mrs. Ramsay bent down and began stacking newspaper-wrapped dishes in a carton. "I hate saying good-bye," she said, "even when we'll be as close as Milwaukee."

"I hope you'll like it in Milwaukee," Carrie said.

"Oh, Lord, I hope so." Then Mrs. Ramsay stood up and began taking glasses out of the cupboard. "Look," she said, "before I pack all these, would you like a glass of lemonade? We could take it out in the yard where the chaos is somewhat less total."

"Aren't you busy?"

"I am *so* busy that half an hour isn't going to make any difference."

172

Carrie watched while she made powdered lemonade. They took it out onto the back steps and sat down.

At the far end of the yard an enormous sunflower was in full bloom. "That's Noah's," Mrs. Ramsay said. "He planted it for the birds."

Carrie thought of a sunflower she and Tanya had planted once in a pot on Tanya's fire escape—long ago when they were children in Hyde Park.

"A lot has changed this year," she said quietly.

Mrs. Ramsay nodded. "For me, too."

Mrs. Ramsay seemed so much as she always had that for a minute Carrie permitted herself to doubt the rumor. Briefly she thought of mentioning it to Mrs. Ramsay. They would smile together at its absurdity. Everything would be as it always had been, nothing changed. But Carrie waited a minute more and knew she would never do it. She was certain somehow that the rumor was true. Whatever she felt now about Mrs. Ramsay would have to include everything she knew.

"I know you'll keep on painting," Mrs. Ramsay was saying. "I want to hear what you're doing when you find time to write."

Carrie nodded.

"I never had a better student, Carrie."

Carrie looked down at the old porch step between her feet. "I never had a better teacher."

She drew in her breath sharply. "Or friend," she said. She stared resolutely at the porch step so that the tears that were in her eyes were hidden. "You will always be my friend, Mrs. Ramsay. Nothing could ever change that.''

She meant it. The rumor, the thing Mrs. Ramsay had done that she couldn't understand—that mattered, of course. But she loved Mrs. Ramsay, and so she had to make room for it.

Mrs. Ramsay stood up and reached for Carrie's empty glass. ''That's how I feel,'' she said. ''Exactly.''

Her mother was the only one at home. She was sitting on the screened porch addressing invitations to a cocktail party, with a glass of iced tea on one side and a neat stack of envelopes on the other. ''Carrie,'' she called, ''I talked to Mrs. Gooch. She has another lamp. They were a pair, and she just happens to have the other one. Aren't we lucky?''

Carrie came out onto the porch. ''I ought to pay for it,'' she said. ''I broke it more or less on purpose.''

''You did?'' Her mother looked up, and Carrie saw in her face for the first time in several months the old look of apprehension, the hospital look.

''I got mad and threw a pillow. It hit the lamp.''

''I'm sure you didn't mean to break it.''

''I meant to throw the pillow.''

''I'll bet it was the heat,'' her mother said. ''This weather tends to make people irritable.'' Then she smiled hopefully up at Carrie as if she wanted Carrie to agree.

Carrie bent down and put her arms around her mother. Doing it felt strange. She couldn't remember when she'd last hugged her mother.

"I'm going to fix a sandwich. Do you want me to bring you anything?"

"No, dear. Thanks," her mother said. She patted Carrie's arm.

And then Carrie went out into the kitchen. She put her head against the refrigerator door and cried.

◦34◦

During the next week the dog days began, the weary, hot last days of August. The lawns in Northpoint lay brown and flattened. Twilight came earlier and, with it, crickets singing their end-of-summer song.

The Recreation Center closed the week before Labor Day, so Carrie's job ended. Moira quit at the same time. Duncan was already going to soccer practice at Sylvester each hot afternoon.

The days were sweltering. All night the air was thick. Labor Day weekend was the hottest one in twenty-six years, the paper said—95 degrees by 8:00 a.m.

And then one day it turned cool.

Carrie woke shivering. She pulled up the sheet she'd kicked off in the night and, before she opened her eyes, she knew it was fall. The air was crisp as cellophane. The leaves started to turn and school began.

A month ago. Already she'd spent a month in ninth

grade. Carrie hitched up her book bag and watched the elevator button blink "23." It wasn't bad in ninth grade, she thought. So far, at least, she didn't mind it.

The elevator shivered to a stop. The door slid open. Carrie stepped out. She walked along the corridor to the waiting room outside Dr. Ross's office and stood looking out the window at the Prudential Building and at the lake beyond it. She knew what she wanted to tell him today.

"I know why I got sick," she said quietly after she had sat down across from him. "I think I know. This morning during English I suddenly understood."

Dr. Ross leaned back and Carrie looked from his face to the desk. She studied its scarred surface thoughtfully.

"It's not mysterious. It's what we have said before, that for some people growing up is especially hard. For Moira it isn't. For me it is. All at once it made sense."

She looked up at him, then back at the desk. "I don't think that's a cop-out. I think it's just true."

He didn't reply. She gazed past his head at the patch of blue sky beyond the window and tried to find words to explain why she suddenly knew this. A cloud was moving out across the lake and, just under it, there was a tiny flash of silver—a plane going somewhere away from Chicago.

"This morning I thought to myself, you never *have* liked anything to change. Then I realized that for a long time I pretended it never would have to. It got harder to pretend. Finally I couldn't do it. That's all."

On the way home Carrie thought about what she'd said. It was like fitting the first pieces of a puzzle together. There were other things she didn't understand yet. There were still loose pieces to sort and fit and think about. It would take time, but she thought that she could do it.

Sophie was snapping beans at the kitchen sink when she came in. Carrie could smell dinner cooking. "Little Sara Meyers was looking for you," Sophie said. "She's waiting out back."

Carrie got herself a handful of potato chips and went out.

Sara was squatting beside the fish pond. "Did your father take the fish out already? I can't see them," she said.

"Not yet. Watch."

"I've *been* watching."

"Well, watch a little longer." Carrie knelt down on the grass beside the little girl. She offered her a potato chip.

"Where've you been?" Sara said, chewing.

"To see my doctor."

"Are you sick?"

"I don't think so."

"Hey, look! A fish!" Sara exclaimed, and immediately she was on her knees, leaning halfway into the pond.

"You have to keep quiet," Carrie whispered. And then she said, "Here, Sara. Crumble this onto the water." She handed her another potato chip.

Obediently Sara broke the potato chip into bits. "Now," Carrie said "watch what I do." And then she leaned far out over the water and gently she whistled.

Sara crouched beside her, transfixed. "What are you doing?"

"Watch." Carrie whistled again so softly her breath barely ruffled the surface.

"Oh, look!" Sara whispered.

The fish rose, swimming toward the surface. Carrie settled back on her haunches and grinned. "Goldfish language," she said. "I learned it when I was eight years old."

"Magic!" said Sara.

Carrie nodded. "That's what I used to think."

"Not now?"

"Not any more."

"I think so. I think it's magic."

"Well, look," Carrie said, "then I'll give it to you. It can be your very own language from now on."

"Really?" Sara looked at her with shining eyes. "Honest?"

"Really. And when it stops seeming magical to you, you can give it to someone else."

"It'll never stop," Sara said.

"It will."

Sara looked at her doubtfully. Then she gripped the rocks that ringed the pond and leaned gingerly out over the water. She blew at the surface, sending the remaining crumbs scudding toward the center. Carrie followed them with her eyes.

And that was when she saw the island. She caught her

breath, then almost laughed. It looked just as it always had—a pile of rocks in the middle of the pond.

"There it is," she said quietly.

"What is?" Sara asked.

"The island," said Carrie. "It's been there all along."

Sara looked at her curiously, then went back to blowing at the water. How strange, Carrie thought, that it had taken her so long to recognize it.

After Sara went home, Carrie crumbled the rest of the potato chips onto the water. The sun had almost set. The air was growing cold. She gazed at the crumbs growing soggy and at the pile of rocks in the middle of the pond. Really, she thought, it was a very small island. She could easily reach it with the handle of a broom.

After a while she looked back at the house. There were lights in the kitchen, lights upstairs, and she could see lights across the street in the Spanglers' windows. Hugging her sweater around her, she turned and walked toward them.

ABOUT THE AUTHOR

Zibby Oneal is a lecturer in the Department of English at the University of Michigan. She has written several books for younger children. She lives in Ann Arbor, Michigan, with her husband, son, and daughter.